MYTHOLOGICAL
HEROES

MYTHOLOGICAL HEROES

M. R. PADILLA

© EDIMAT BOOKS Ltd. London
is an affiliate of Edimat Libros S.A.
C/ Primavera, 35 Pol. Ind. El Malvar
Arganda del Rey - 28500 (Madrid) Spain
E-mail: edimat@edimat.es

Title: *Mythological Heroes*
Author: *M. R. Padilla*

ISBN: 84-9794-026-1
Legal Deposit: M-48226-2004

PRINTED IN SPAIN

PROLOGUE

To define the meaning of 'myth', 'legend', or 'mythology' is more difficult than it may at first seem; such a definition cannot satisfy everybody at once. It would be wrong to say that a myth is the same as a fable or an allegory; it is something much more complex, yet at the same time, simpler. These terms have a much wider sense, while the focus of study also depends on the person who carries it out.

For example, a psychologist would find an allegory within the myth or look for symbols relating to the human soul and reflections of a collective unconscious. A philologist would be more concerned with the language, the phonetics, the metaphors, and the origin of the myth than its overall meaning. A historian, on the other hand, would give more attention to the chronology of events and to how they reflect the society that created them. A philosopher would look for primitive, pre-logic and dramatic thought, while an artist would use mythology as a source of continuous inspiration.

Avoiding reference to academic studies, we could say that the most generalised definition of a myth is a tale or narration, which in most cases contains symbolic and extraordinary elements and, more definitively, presents a tale which is usually of a dramatic, exemplary nature. The collection of these tales forms a 'tribal history' and the cultural baggage of a society. They originated in prehistoric times and have been passed orally from generation to generation. Their veracity is accepted by all, and they are commonly used for providing examples or teaching morals.

In fact, and not forgetting their religious nature, myths provide us with many of the first interpretations of the world – an illustration of the world through the narration of marvellous and exemplary events. The subjects that mythology deals with are those which are particularly interesting to the community, providing logical explanations for the primordial aspects of our world, such as life, death, and the origins of all things, or addressing moral issues, such as loyalty, friendship, love, or punishment.

The greatest virtue of myths, in my humble opinion, is that of introducing the aspect of doubt as to the existence of the Olympic gods, the heroes, or the monsters and questioning whether the stories really happened as they are told.

This book offers the reader a wide selection of the most important, representative, evocative, and even some of the more unknown and enigmatic myths. We have included, wherever possible, as we did in the previous volume, brief analyses of the myths in order to provide the reader with a more comprehensive study and a fuller understanding of each one. The book also includes a series of annotations in the last pages, in the form of a genealogical tree that can be of help to demonstrate points of reference.

To conclude this prologue, I would like to indicate the one thing that all myths and legends have in common: the variety of versions found of each one. In some cases, we have printed only one version, and where we have judged it useful, we have included more than one.

I

THE LEGENDS
OF THE OLYMPIC GODS

> *The gods themselves,*
> *Humbling their deities to love, have taken*
> *The shapes of beasts upon them: Jupiter*
> *Became a bull, and bellow'd.*
>
> Shakespeare

> *Be brave, gentle maiden! Fear not queasiness;*
> *I, although in appearance a bull, am Jupiter of the heavens;*
> *My form I change as I desire.*
>
> Moschus

1. THE LOVES OF ZEUS

The legends that tell of the King of the gods are almost all tales of his love adventures. Apart from the children he fathered with nymphs descended from the Titans or the gods (Hermes with Maia, the daughter of Atlas; Apollo and Artemis with Leto, daughter of the Titans, Koios and Phoibe; and Dionysus with Semele), the unfaithful god also loved many mortal women. The following are four interesting illustrations of the amorous talents of the great god.

• The legend of Io and the gadfly

According to legend, Io was a priestess of the city of Argos, daughter of King Inachus in some versions and of King Iasos of Argos in others. Zeus was seduced by her beauty, and so that his jealous wife would not suspect that he had been unfaithful, he turned Io into a lovely cow. His wife Hera was not fooled by the trick and asked him to consecrate the animal, which he did, and the cow was given into the care of Argos, a giant with a hundred eyes, who only ever closed fifty of them while he slept. But Zeus sent Hermes to rescue Io, which he did by playing the giant to sleep with his flute and then killing him. When Hera found out, she gathered up the hundred eyes and put them on the tail of the peacock, to serve as a permanent reminder of the heinous crime. Then, in revenge, she sent a gadfly to sting Io and pursue her throughout the world.

Io spent several months wandering all over Greece as a cow, fleeing from the sting of the gadfly. When she crossed the Bosporus Strait (the ford of the cow), she found Prometheus chained to a rock on a mountain in the Caucasus, who according to Aeschylus' tale, predicted her a happy fate. Io therefore decided to go to Egypt, where she recovered her human form and gave birth to Epaphus.

Analysis of the legend

Io was identified with the goddess Iris and, after her death, with the goddess Luna, represented as a woman with golden horns.

This legend is a beautiful allegory in which Io personifies the Moon, wandering without rest from one place to another; Argos represents the sky, whose starry eyes incessantly follow the movement of the moon; and Hermes is the rain, whose arrival makes the stars disappear, metaphorically killing the giant Argos.

• The legend of the kidnapping of Europa

Europa was the direct descendent of Io and Zeus. Her parents, Agenor, grandson of Epaphus and Telephassa, and her brothers were Phoenix, Phineus, Cadmus and Cilix.

Europa was as beautiful as the morning, with smooth white skin. One day, she was playing by the edge of the sea with her friends when Zeus saw her and immediately fell in love with her. To avoid Hera's jealousy, he turned himself into a white bull with golden horns in the shape of crescent moons, but unthreatening. When Europa saw him, she felt the desire to sit on his back and feel the smoothness of his skin. Suddenly, the divine animal hurled himself out to sea and disappeared, with Europa on his back. Guided by Eros, they arrived at the island of Crete, near to Cortina, where green bananas have grown to commemorate the union of the lovers ever since. Europa bore three children, whose names perpetuate and glorify the legend: Minos, Rhadamanthys, and Sarpedon. Her brothers set out in search of her and founded many colonies on their travels.

Analysis of the legend

This legend, according to the historian Herodotus, is linked to a series of kidnappings of princes and princesses that were in his opinion the motive for the ancient quarrels of war between Asians and Europeans. In his History I and II, he tells that the Phoenicians kidnapped Io, daughter of Inachus, from Argos; and then the Greeks kidnapped Europa; other Greeks took Medea from Colchis; and finally, the Trojan Paris seduced and carried away Helen, wife of King Menelaus of Sparta, to his city, from whence came the ill-fated Homeric war.

The ancient peoples named one of the four parts of the world Europe, in memory of the young Phoenician.

The myth of the seducing bull has, in addition to its gallant tone, a mysterious echo of rituals involving bulls.

• The legend of Danae

Danae was the daughter of Acrisius, King of Argos, and she lived happily with him until the day an oracle predicted that her son would end the life of his grandfather. The King, in fear of his own death, therefore imprisoned the beautiful Danae in a bronze tower.

But Zeus, who had already seen Danae, fell hopelessly in love with her, and refusing to give up the object of his desire, he transformed himself into a fine golden rain that penetrated the cold cell and seduced the young girl. The result of this magical union was a son, Perseus. When Acrisius realised that his daughter was expecting a child, he shut her in a chest and threw it into the sea. The chest was washed up on the shore of the island of Seriphus, reigned over by Polydectes. With the passing of time, Perseus was to return to Argos and fulfil the oracle's prediction.

• The legend of Leda

Leda, the daughter of King Thestios of Aetolia, was living in her father's court when she met Tyndareus, who had lost his kingdom of Sparta.

There are several versions of this legend in existence. One of them tells how Zeus, in love with Leda, turned himself into a beautiful swan and seduced her on the shore of the river Eurotas. By coincidence, Leda also had been with her husband, Tyndareus, that very night. Leda laid an egg from which hatched Helen, Clytemnestra, Castor, and Polydeuces.

Some say that only Helen was Zeus's child; others that Castor and Clytemnestra were the children of Tyndareus, and Helen and Polydeuces were Zeus's children. Castor and Polydeuces were twins, who became known as the Dioscuri, and were later the pride of Sparta.

10

*Since proud Ixion (doomed to feel the tortures
of th'eternal wheel, Bound by the hand of angry Jove)
Received the due rewards of impious love.*

Sophocles

2. THE LEGENDS OF HERA

Hera usually appears in legends as the jealous and vengeful wife. There are few legends in which she is the main character, but here we can see two of those legends in which she is given a different role.

• The legend of Cleobis and Biton

Cydippe, an old priestess of Hera, was on one particular occasion very excited and impatient to set off for a ceremony in the temple of Argos, where she had performed ceremonies for many years, leaving only with the consent of her goddess to get married. Due to her old age and the difficulty of a long and dusty journey, she asked her twin sons, Cleobis and Biton, to harness their two white oxen to the cart. Both sons were anxious to do as their mother wished, but they could find no trace of the beasts.

In order to avoid disappointing their mother, after making her comfortable in the cart, they decided to harness themselves to it, and they set off on the strenuous journey, bearing her to the very doors of the temple, where they were acclaimed by the townspeople in admiration of such a demonstration of goodness and filial devotion.

Cydippe approached the altar and fervently begged the great goddess to recompense her sons for their sacrifice, by conceding them the best reward that she could offer. Having finished the service, the old woman, still very emotional, went to the porch where she had left her sons and found them lying down. The ex-priestess, who had believed them to be asleep after the efforts of the journey, found them to be dead. The Queen of the gods had put them into a deep sleep and transported them to Elysium, the place of eternal happiness, where they could enjoy their well-earned rest during an eternal and pleasant life.

• The legend of Ixion

Ixion, the son of Phlegyas, was a king of the Lapiths, who agreed to marry Dia, the daughter of King Deioneus. But Ixion not only broke his word to his father-in-law by not giving him the valuable gifts he had promised, but prepared a trap for the King in front of his palace, underneath which burned a great coal fire. The trusting Deioneus fell into the fire and was burned. The crime was so terrible that nobody was willing to purge Ixion except Zeus, who went so far as to invite him to eat at his table, offering him nectar and ambrosia, the food of the gods, which grant immortality. Drunk, and far from being grateful for these gifts, Ixion demonstrated his unpleasant character by trying to seduce Hera. So Zeus created a cloud in the exact image of Hera, which he called Nephele. Ixion was too drunk to realise what was going on and went to bed with her. This union produced the first centaur – half man, half horse – who it is said later sired hippo-centaurs with magnesia mares, of which the wisest was Chiron.

Zeus decided that he needed to make an example of Ixion, so he told Hermes to chain him to a forever-turning wheel of fire covered in snakes. This punishment was to represent the eternal punishment of the impious and ungrateful.

Brilliant, like times before, the sun rays resting on you,
Empires have sunk since you were revered
For the first time,
And several rites have blessed our sanctuary.
Dust that covered you for the test that they had to
undergo
Your walls, and you, its destiny will soon be yours!

Hemans

3. ATHENA AND ERICTONIUS' CRIB

• The legend of Erictonius' crib

On one occasion, Poseidon wanted to tease poor Hephaestus, and he told him that Athena fancied him and waited for the day when he would wildly make love to her. So it was, one day, Athena came to see how the task she had entrusted to Hephaestus was progressing. He had declared that he would not charge her anything, that he would forge her arms for free, for his love for her. Athena didn't suspect anything; she thought that Hephaestus was of good heart. When she went into the forge, Hephaestus leapt for her, overwhelmed by his excitement. Once Athena managed to free herself from him, Hephaestus ejaculated on her leg. Disgusted, she cleaned herself with a tuft of wool which she threw to the Earth, fertilising it. Mother Earth refused to give birth to a child that had been destined for Athena, and thus the goddess accepted responsibility for the boy and called him *Erictonius*. He was trusted to the guard of the three daughters of *Cecrops*: *Agraulas*, *Herse*, and *Pandrosus*. The boy was left in a closed basket, and it was recommended to the three sisters that they should not open the basket under any circumstances. They were victims to their curiosity, however, and they opened the basket. They saw before them a boy surrounded by two serpents. They were so shaken that they threw it from the heights of the citadel of Athens. Later, after Erictonius had become king of the city, he began the cult of Athena and initiated the Panathenean Festival. He was succeeded by his son *Pandeon*.

In another version, it is told how Erictonius' crib was delivered to Agraulas. Hermes (in other versions, Apollo) fell in love with Herse, the youngest sister, and bribed Agraulus to intervene on his behalf. She took the money, but didn't do anything. Hermes, angered, turned her into stone and seduced Herse, who was to give him two sons, *Cephalus* and *Ceryx*. Later, the two sisters, curious to know what was in the basket that Athena had entrusted to

13

Agraulus, opened it and saw to their horror a boy with a serpent's tail instead of legs. In order to be rid of this horrible vision, they threw it from the top of the Acropolis.

Athena felt so grieved that she let an enormous rock fall on the place where the basket had fallen, resulting in the formation of the mountain Lycabettos. As for the white crow that had brought the sad news, she changed its colour to black and prohibited all crows that later visited the Acropolis. Since then, the crow has been a sign of misfortune.

Erictonius sought refuge beneath Athena's cloak, and gaining her affection, she brought him up like a mother. The image of Erictonius was installed among the stars as the constellation Auriga, since it was he who introduced the four-horse chariot.

> There remains a prayer for me to offer.
> Your quiver contains
> more than nine arrows: stretch your bow, aim here!
> I can see it, I can see it tenuously through a cloud.
> Artemis you are more than pious:
> My children will not hear the fatal tolling!

> W.S. Landor

4. THE LEGENDS OF ARTEMIS

Here are two legends about the same goddess; together they reveal the two faces of this deity. The first presents us with Artemis, the cruel and vengeful goddess of hunting, and the second with Diana, her Roman equivalent, goddess of the moon, a virgin, but in love.

• The legend of Niobe

Niobe, daughter of *Tantalus* and wife of *Amphion*, boasted to all of her fertility and the beauty of her fourteen chil-

14

dren: seven sons and seven daughters. Furthermore, she ridiculed Leto, or Latona to the Romans, since she had only two: Apollo and Artemis. Both, indignant at Niobe's presumption, killed her children one by one. Apollo shot his poisoned arrows at the seven sons and Artemis hers at the daughters. Only one daughter escaped the massacre, but, terrorised, her face retained a mortal paleness for the rest of her life, earning her the name Cloris, 'Greenish'.

Niobe, hearing the desperate screams of her children, came out of her palace and saw with horror what had happened. She was so petrified that, in order to escape the horrible spectacle of her children's bodies in agony, she looked to the skies while tears flowed from her eyes and begged the gods for clemency.

Jupiter took pity on her, turning her into a rock, but her tears continued to flow, so deep was her grief, forming a fountain. That rock can be found on Mount Sipilos.

This allegory explains how Niobe, the mother who represents cold, harsh, and proud winter, sees how Apollo, the rays of the Sun, kills her sons, the winter months. Her tears are symbols of the natural melting that comes with spring when winter's pride has been melted.

• The legend of Endymeon

With the falling of the day, Diana rose in her lunar chariot and drove her silvery steeds across the dark sky. After greeting the stars, she tended to descend to observe the Earth, so during the night she appeared at her most enchanting and mysterious.

One night, while she descended to contemplate the Earth, she made out in the distance a young, handsome shepherd who lay sleeping. The goddess could not resist the temptation of approaching to contemplate him from closer by. Perplexed, she admired his beauty, and she soon felt her heart beating with something more than admiration. She then lowered herself and kissed the smooth lips of the shepherd, who upon feeling the gentle brushing half-opened his eyes and contemplated with admiration the beauty of his visitor. Although the speed of the goddess led him to believe that it had been a dream with just the Moon having been before him, a flame was lit in his heart.

The following night, the same thing occurred, and the love between them grew. The goddess Diana, however, had begged her father, Jupiter, that she be allowed to remain single and a virgin. Thus, Diana decided that, in order to eternally enjoy the company of her lover without breaking her word, she should induce Endymeon into an eternal sleep. And that is precisely what she did, transporting him to a sacred cave in Mount Latmos. There, the goddess went every night to contemplate, enraptured, the beloved countenance and to seal with a kiss the unconscious lips.

This beautiful story of Diana, the Moon goddess, and Endymeon, the handsome shepherd, has inspired poets throughout the ages.

> *Scaling the sky's curve,*
> *I walk over mountains and waves,*
> *Leaving my tunic in the sea foam;*
> *My steps light the clouds in flame, caves*
> *Are full of my brilliant presence and the air*
> *Leaves the green earth open to my embrace.*

Shelley

5. THE LEGENDS OF APOLLO

Apollo is one of the most represented gods in the legends. Given his wayward, amorous talents, he appears in many legends of romance. Curiously, Apollo is also the only male god, if we ignore Zeus's affair with Ganymede, that sought company from his own sex. There are two legends in this respect, as follows:

• The legend of Hyacinth

Hyacinth was a smart, handsome, young man whose favours were disputed by several gods and men. But it was Apollo and no other that succeeded in wooing the beautiful mortal.

On one occasion, when they were having a good time together, they decided to throw discus. Hyacinth started the game by throwing first. The young man, in addition to his beauty, was a good athlete and threw a long distance. Apollo took his turn and threw in the same instant as *Zephyr,* the East Wind, appeared. By chance, Zephyr was also in love with the handsome Hyacinth, and jealous that he had chosen to be with Apollo rather than him, he diverted the discus thrown by the god with a blow, directing it towards the boy's forehead, killing him instantly.

Apollo tried in vain to stop the blood flowing from his playmate's wound. Faced with this awful disgrace, Apollo was stunned and inconsolable. In an attempt to keep alive in some way the memory of his beloved friend, he transformed the blood spilt on the ground into a purple lily-shaped flower in whose petals he inscribed the word 'ay', which in Greek means 'What a shame!', or represents the first letter of his name in Greek: 'Y'. Meanwhile, repentant Zephyr, realising too late the fatal consequence of his jealousy, flew inconsolably around the sad place, taking exquisitely delicate care of the flowers that had sprung up from the handsome youth's blood.

Some mythologists contend the hypothesis that this allegory, in which the young mortal's life is cut short at the prime of his life and is transformed into a flower, was born from the archaic practice of human sacrifice. During such rituals, the immolated victim's blood would flow into the earth in order to fertilise it.

• The legend of Cypress

After poor Hyacinth died from the mortal blow of the discus, Apollo felt lonely once more. To forget the sad events and console his heart, the god went in search of Cypress' companionship: a young, daring hunter. Both of them were very happy, but one day Cypress killed Apollo's pet stag by accident. Cypress was so upset by his terrible mistake that it consumed him until he died.

Grief-stricken, Apollo transformed the body of his friend into a cypress tree, which became from that moment onwards the beautiful shade that shelters the graves of those who have been deeply loved in life.

II

LEGENDS OF LOVE AND MUTATIONS

> *Again she dy'd, nor yet her lord reprov'd;*
> *What could she say, but that too well he lov'd?*
> *One last farewell she spoke, which scarce he heard;*
> *So soon she drop'd, so sudden disappear'd.*

Ovid

1. ORPHEUS AND EURYDICE

The power of love

This is a legend of tragic love, an unrivalled love that was so strong, it could challenge Death. Such is the story of *Orpheus*, legendary Greece's most virtuous musician and poet, and of *Eurydice*, a beautiful dryad.

Orpheus was the son of *Oeagrus*, the King of Thrace, and the muse *Calliope*, 'of the beautiful voice'. It is told that Apollo presented him with the seven-string lyre, to which he added two more in honour of the nine Muses. In appreciation, the Muses taught him to play sweet songs on it. The young man learnt swiftly, surpassing his teachers in skill and talent. His mastery was beyond even that of Apollo.

When Orpheus sang his sweet, moving melodies, rocks cried with emotion, rivers stopped their flow to hear him, and wild cats followed him tamely. Such was his power that on the Argonaut's expedition, united to discover the world, he was able to conquer the seduction of the sirens' songs and neutralise its evil power.

On his return, he met the beautiful Eurydice and fell madly in love with her. He courted her with beautiful songs that the nymph could not resist, and she agreed to wed him. They lived very happily for the first days of their marriage, but bad fortune had it that Eurydice bumped into *Aristaeus* on one of her strolls. Seduced by her beauty, he tried to rape her. Eurydice managed to escape his clutches and fled terrified. During her escape, however, she stood on a snake that bit her heel.

The fatal bite caused the unfortunate Eurydice to suffer intense pain before she died. Her spirit was then taken to the sombre underworld, leaving her beloved Orpheus utterly devastated.

Orpheus' intense grief as a result of the loss of his adored wife prevented him from playing the happy melodies that he used to, only capable of singing heartrending laments, which broke the hearts of all those who listened. And there was one moment when his suffering was so unbearable, he set off for Mount Olympus and requested an audience with Zeus. He implored the great god in such a way – asking that she be returned to him – that Zeus, profoundly moved by this incredibly beautiful love, gave him permission to descend into the world of Hades, after warning him of the danger he would put himself in. But Orpheus was not scared and left ready to perform such a task.

While he descended into the Underworld, Orpheus couldn't hide his happiness at the prospect of seeing Eurydice again. On his way, he came across the River Styx. There was only one way to cross the river: pay *Charon*, the ferryman, but since Orpheus didn't have any money, he played his lyre and charmed the old ferryman into letting him cross without paying. Then the terrible *Cerberus* appeared, ready to tear him to pieces as he passed. Orpheus started to play an irresistible melody and pacified the beast into letting him pass. He continued playing, and the melancholic notes of love spread all around Tartarus, reaching even the most hidden corners in the depths, where the condemned souls stopped their painful labour and hushed their spine-chilling groans and laments.

This was how the virtuous Orpheus reached the throne of the king of these dark domains, Hades, and his wife Persephone. He informed them of the purpose of his daring visit. At first, the dark king refused to concede such privilege to him, but Persephone, profoundly moved by his love, interceded on his behalf. Hades consented for Eurydice to leave his kingdom, but on one condition: he had to go first, and most importantly, he could not turn around to look at her until they had reached the land of the living.

It seemed an easy enough condition to Orpheus, and he accepted it happily. He started to walk while playing a cheerful melody while Eurydice followed him full of joy. As they climbed the narrow path out, Orpheus started to wonder if it all wasn't just some beautiful dream or, even worse, a trick by Hades to get rid of him, and when he looked round to see the beautiful face of his beloved, he wouldn't find anything more than blackness. They were just one metre from the border between the two worlds when Orpheus, unable to bear his doubt any longer, turned his head. There was Eurydice, as beautiful as ever, but as soon as he saw her, she started to be pulled back, and her serene body turned into a scream of panic as she felt herself absorbed by that evil force. Orpheus, in despair, stretched out his arms in an attempt to grab her, but it was too late, and Eurydice disappeared forever.

All hope gone, totally devastated by the repeated loss, Orpheus couldn't stop tormenting himself that his impatience and suspicion had prevented, with just one step to go, the miracle of meeting his Eurydice. His attempt had failed, and now he wouldn't have another opportunity. The disconsolate musician returned to Thrace, and from that moment on he only picked up his lyre to play funereal melodies that made both people and plants or even rocks cry in suffering. Even so, Orpheus received several offers of marriage, but faithful to the memory of his wife, he rejected them all.

It was around that time that Dionysus conquered Thrace and wanted Orpheus to honour him with a beautiful, happy melody for the maenads to dance their wild dance to. But Orpheus refused, because he only honoured Apollo, and moreover, he predicted for the people of Thrace the evil of the Dionysian sacrifice. Dionysus, irritated and offended, incited the maenads to tear Orpheus to pieces in Deium, Macedonia. That was where Orpheus served as a priest in a temple of Apollo. The maenads broke into the building, caught Orpheus, and in the delirium of their madness, killed their husbands who were joining Orpheus in his worship of Apollo. They dismembered the unfortunate musician and disposed of his limbs in the River Hebrus. His head floated downriver to the Island of Lesbos. It is told how the head sang a beautiful melody, because he joyfully thought that at last he would be reunited with his beloved.

The mourning Muses gathered together the pieces of Orpheus' body and buried them in Leibethra at the foot of Mount Olympus, where it is said that nightingales now sing more sweetly than in any other place on Earth. His head, however, was buried in a cave at Antissa, consecrated paradoxically to Dionysus. There it prophesised day and night, until Apollo, tired of seeing his temples in Delphi or Gryneium deserted, ordered him to be quiet. The lyre, upon petition by the Muses, was placed by Zeus among the other constellations.

Analysis of the myth

Orpheus is one of the oldest and richest characters in Greek mythology. He has had a great influence on poets and artists. Numerous musical works have been inspired by this beautiful myth; we only have to think of "Orpheus" by Claudio Monteverdi, performed in Italy at the start of the seventeenth century, in which he tried to sentimentalise by giving it a happy ending. It has also been performed in the-

atre; Jean Cocteau's "Orpheus" was first a tragedy, performed in 1926, and years later, in 1949 to be precise, it
was produced as a film. This myth has also inspired sculptors and painters: Tintoretto, Corot, Bruegel, and Rubens,
among others. All of them coincide in presenting Orpheus
as the man that brings civilisation to savages, teaching
them the art of peace.

Christian artists saw in Orpheus the referential hero of
peace and harmony, for eternity; he who confronted death
fearlessly and returned to the land of the living. This allegory transformed, in turn, into an important symbol for
psychoanalysis: by turning to look at Eurydice he confronts
the forbidden to see the invisible.

But Orpheus has also been thought of as the introduction
to the Orphic myths. One assumes that when he travelled to
Egypt with the Argonauts, the Osiris mysteries began,
which inspired later the creation of the Orphic mysteries of
Eleusis. Orphic followers worshipped the god Apollo. They
abstained from blood sacrifices, practiced a life of purity,
refrained from eating meat, and believed in eternal life –
the Great Beyond, and like Pythagorean followers, the
transmigration of the soul.

According to Orphic theogony, the world was created
from a great egg: the top part turned into the sky and the
lower into the Earth. Later, the creation gods appeared, and
finally, Zeus fathered *Zagreus,* who ruled the world. And
even though his enemies tore him to pieces, Zeus managed
to resuscitate him, joining together all the limbs. Thus life,
death, and resurrection were represented.

This Orphic myth was idealised to such an extent that it
was identified with Christ, the good shepherd who calms
storms and pacifies the waters; the man who dies and
returns from hell.

> *But her voice is still living immortal,*
> *The same you have frequently heard,*
> *In your rambles in valleys and forests,*
> *Repeating your ultimate word.*

Saxe

2. ECHO AND NARCISSUS

Unrequited love

This is the legend of *Narcissus*, a young man whose beauty was captivating, and a cheerful nymph called *Echo*. Narcissus was the son of the river god *Cephissus*, in Phocis, and the nymph *Leiriope*. When his mother went to see the oracle *Teiresias*, he predicted: "Narcissus will only live if he doesn't come to know himself."

Narcissus' beauty was such that all who had the misfortune of contemplating him fell in love with him, but he was always indifferent to their displays of admiration and scornful of the continuous insinuations of the numerous young women that pursued him, captivated by his beauty.

One day, a nymph called Echo was passing by a meadow where Narcissus lay, engrossed in a pleasant dream. Once she saw his beauty, Echo fell madly in love with him. She hid herself and contemplated his charm until he woke up. Seeing that the object of her desire was going to escape from her sight without her being able to do anything about it, she walked forward, stepping on a stick that broke with a dry snap. Alerted to her presence, Narcissus asked,

–"Who's there?"
–*"There?", replied Echo.*

When Echo was in the service of the goddess Hera, she used to distract her with continuous chatter while Zeus' lovers escaped. When Hera realised the deceit, she punished Echo by condemning her with the following words: "You will always say the last word, but never the first."

–"Who are you? Why don't you come out?", insisted Narcissus.
–*"Come out?", repeated Echo.*
–"But, where are you? I can't see you."
–*"See you."*
–"Well, I can't see you. Why don't you come out?"
–*"Come out?"*
–"I'm sick of this game. I'm going."

Echo and Narcissus.

–"I'm going," said Echo, when she wanted to say exactly the opposite and seeing that her beloved was escaping her, she came out to meet him.

But Narcissus, tired of their stupid conversation, found no lure in the nymph to stay with her and scornfully departed. Echo then wandered lost to a cliff, where she languished in love and humiliation, until all that remained was her voice. So it was that even dead, in some parts of the Earth, you can still hear Echo's voice repeating the last thing she hears.

Echo's sisters pleaded for justice to Nemesis, the goddess of revenge and daughter of the Night. The goddess listened to the indignant nymphs' petition and decided to avenge Echo and the other desperate admirers. Thus, fulfilling Teiresias' prophecy, she made Narcissus satiate his thirst in a spring while he was hunting.

When Narcissus knelt down to drink, he saw his reflection in the crystal waters of the spring. It seemed to him that in all his life, he had never seen such a handsome face, hair so beautiful, or sweeter features. And he continued contemplating the reflection without realising that it was his own until he decided to reach out and touch the incredibly beautiful being. But when he touched the water, the image disappeared, and Narcissus felt the stab of pain of unrequited love.

After a while, the image returned, but as soon as he stroked it, it disappeared again. And thus, time and again, until the suffering admirer decided that if he couldn't have the handsome creature, he would at least watch it until he was filled with its beauty. Several days and nights went by, and Narcissus stayed there, without moving, so obsessed by his own image that he forgot to eat or drink. Little by little, his body languished away waiting to be responded to by this unattainable love; his legs turned into roots, his arms and body into a stem and leaves, and his handsome face into a beautiful flower, which since then has taken his name.

So it was that Echo was avenged. Narcissus languished to death for unrequited love, although unsuspecting that it was love for himself.

Analysis of the myth

The Narcissus (from Greek *Narke,* which means 'narcosis') was known in Greece for its capacity to produce sleep, even for the gods. This happened to Persephone when she fell asleep from its perfume, making it easy for Hades to kidnap her and take her to his underworld.

In ancient times, there was a spring in Thespia called Narcissus that fell on a rock causing an echo. Narcissus flowers in Spring, precisely where there are springs in which they enjoy their reflection to later wither in winter. Considering these points, it is easy to comprehend this interesting myth, but the enormous repercussion of this myth, both in the world of art and literature and in psychology, should be stressed.

Narcissus has inspired writers of such standing as Oscar Wilde or Paul Valery, and he has been the subject matter for philosophers such as Gaston Bachelard, who states that water was a mirror in which an idealised 'I' is reflected that doesn't correspond with the real image. Nevertheless, the term 'narcissism' wasn't coined until 1899, by the psychologist P. Naecke. Sigmund Freud included the concept of narcissism in his theory on the sexual behaviour of human beings.

Narcissism is the falling in love with yourself and, definitively, the idea of pleasure as that which comes from your own interior 'I'.

> *Oh, Aphrodite, kind and beautiful,*
> *That your will you can impose.*
> *Oh, listen to a sculptor's plea,*
> *And bring my work to life!*

Andrew Lang

3. PYGMALION AND GALATEA

The artist in love

This is the incredible story of a king of Cyprus called *Pygmalion*, a legendary monarch who had the marvellous gift of sculpting. His skill was such that he could transform an amorphous stone into a truly beautiful piece of art. With just a few strikes of the hammer and chisel, the perfect strokes of a new sculpture could be divined.

Pygmalion could shape or sculpture any object, and he did so with such mastery, his works seemed to be alive: birds looked about to take flight; flowers seemed to flutter in the wind; and animals gave the impression of breathing. But the objects that produced the greatest pleasure, without a doubt, were his sculptures inspired by the gods, satisfying the deities tremendously.

The virtuous king spent whole days working in his workshop. He hardly had time for anything else, and so he remained single. Some people swore that he didn't marry to have more time for sculpting. But one day, he decided to forge the image of a beautiful woman. For such a task he searched for the most beautiful stone he had, a rosy marble, and he started to sculpt. After a few hours, a beautiful woman's body was already starting to take shape. Pygmalion was so motivated by the first results that he continued working. He continued for two days and two nights, and finally, he finished his work, the most beautiful that he had ever created. His experienced hands caressed the rosy face of the stone woman, and he admired the perfection of her features to the last detail. The love he felt for his piece of art had been growing little by little, blow after blow of the hammer, and now Pygmalion felt deeply in love with her.

He decided to give her a name and called her *Galatea*. From that moment on, the enamoured artist was unable to sculpt again. He felt so bewitched by his masterpiece, he stopped eating and drinking. He spent hours watching her, caressing her, talking to her of love – this very new feeling that had blossomed in his heart.

And then one day, he embraced her and cried bitterly while imploring Aphrodite, the goddess of love, to give her life. The goddess pitied Pygmalion, since he had finally become snared by the nets of love and wished to abandon his life of celibacy. So it was she blew life into Galatea; Pygmalion's embrace gave warmth to her frozen body, and the bitter tears of his love, rather than bounce off the cold marble, found the warm touch of a body in which life was awakening. And Pygmalion cried again, but this time from happiness at seeing his work come to life, transformed into the most beautiful woman he had ever seen.

Pygmalion and Galatea married, and from their union was born *Paphos,* founder of the Cyprian city that took the same name. Later, it was the city where a famous sanctuary was built in honour of Aphrodite, the goddess that made the love of an artist and his work come true.

Analysis of the myth

Pygmalion, like Narcissus, has inspired many artists, sculptors, musicians, and writers, especially Ovid in his "Metamorphoses". Jean-Jacques Rousseau wrote "Pygmalion", an opera that was performed in Paris in 1775. Later, Cherubini gave his version of the story of Pygmalion in an opera that was performed in Paris in 1804. Girondet, the famous French painter at the start of the nineteenth century, painted "Pygmalion and Galatea", and half a century later, the sculptor Falconet sculpted in marble a very beautiful piece that depicted Pygmalion at the foot of Galatea at the moment she came to life. The art critic of that time, Diderot, adopted this work with great enthusiasm.

In the literary world, the myth of Pygmalion inspired the work of George Bernard Shaw, the famous Irish writer at the start of the twentieth century. Shaw, an ingenious, satirical writer, created a modern Pygmalion that, as the consequence of a bet, teaches a poor, illiterate flower seller how to pronounce proper English, that is, English upper-class pronunciation. The girl's progress surprises the teacher, whom she eventually surpasses in charm and diction. The feeling of love that unites Pygmalion to his ward is very ambiguous, since it presents the problem of the artist who is more in love with his creation than the actual creature herself.

Just as with Narcissus and Tantalus, the myth of Pygmalion has served to denominate a certain human behaviour, forming part of the language of daily life. We call the artist that falls in love with his own work 'Pygmalion'.

> *"Sweet! For your love", cried he, "I would ply the waves,*
> *Although the foam were fire and the waves burnt with flames.*
> *I fear not the waves if in them you are sustained,*
> *Nor do I waver before the hissing of the sea."*

Edwin Arnold

4. HERO AND LEANDER

Love against the tides

This is the legend of a tragic love. It is the story of *Hero,* a beautiful priestess of the goddess Aphrodite, and *Leander*, a handsome, young man from Abydos.

Hero was given to the service of the goddess by her father when she was still a girl. When she reached the appropriate age, she began spending most of her time at the temple worshipping her goddess. The rest of the time she spent at her lodgings, at the top of a solitary tower by the sea, where she lived with just her ancient nurse for company.

Years went by, only increasing Hero's beauty, and the fame of her good looks spread all around the region from her home city, Sestos, as far as Hellespont and Abydos. This was the quiet city where the young man Leander lived, the most valiant and handsome among all young men, and like all the rest of them, Leander burned with desire to see the tremendously enchanting priestess.

He had the opportunity some weeks later, with the excuse of the festival in honour of the goddess Aphrodite, in which all young men and women of the region were invited to participate. When Leander entered the goddess' temple along with his companions, his eyes avidly sought out the attractive priestess. His search was compensated for by the vision of the most beautiful of creatures. Hero's charms greatly surpassed any description he had heard.

Leander's admiring look met that of the virginal young woman, and she blushed. At this moment, Leander felt Eros' arrow and fell irremediably in love with the young woman. Hero felt exactly the same arrow from the naughty little god, and the flame of love burnt her heart.

Leander managed to approach Hero, and they each confessed the newly-born love they felt for each other. However, Hero refused to consummate that love for fear of her father's anger, having promised him to forever conserve her virginity. But the stubborn lover refused to give in and insisted on arranging a meeting between them, or he would die of love for her.

So Hero explained that although she would agree to seeing him, there was a great obstacle, since he could only reach the tower where she lived by crossing in a rowing boat, since it was on the other side from the Hellespont. The gallant young man, far from being discouraged, told Hero that at nightfall she should light a torch in her room, and he promised her that he would swim across the sea to her solitary tower.

Hero was so moved by her lover's courage that she agreed, full of emotion. That same night, Hero lit a torch. When Leander made out the light given off and that would serve him as a guide, without thinking twice he dove into the cold waters and started to swim vigorously. The brave young man feared nothing while he swam against the current, since the thought of finally being with the beautiful priestess filled him with valour and strength enough to overcome whatever obstacle.

Meanwhile, in the solitary tower and with her heart aflutter, the young woman waited impatiently. When the young swimmer finally arrived, Hero ran to meet him. Their bodies joined in a warm embrace, in which both their hearts beat faster and faster in a whirlwind of effort, anxiety, and passion.

Dawn started to rise from the East when the lovers kissed goodbye. Still worn out after a night of passionate love, they both left, he for Abydos and she for the temple of Aphrodite, anxious for the arrival of the night, they might meet once more. And so, without anyone ever suspecting anything, night after night, Hero lit the torch, and Leander swam against the current to rest in her arms.

But the fearful winter arrived and, with it, ferocious storms. The bad weather did not discourage the courageous lover. Not even Hero's frightened pleas made him change his mind; on the contrary, he laughed at the waves that crashed violently against the coast, promising her that no storm would separate him from her. Thus, one night, defying the force of nature, he plunged into the icy waters and began to swim toward the twinkle of the torch.

Hero had still lit the torch after having prayed to the gods to dissuade her brave lover. Leander fought against the waves while the storm blew with increasingly more violence. The wind blew with such force, the torch went out, and Hero ran to the chimney to relight it. Meanwhile, Leander was gradually losing his strength, and tired out, he implored the gods to help him.

When Hero returned with the relit torch, it was already too late. Not even the sight of the torch could give enough strength to the exhausted swimmer, who drowned like a stone to the bottom of the sea. Hero looked harder to try to make out her lover, but without success. And there she waited all through the night, hoping that Leander was on the opposite shore, healthy and safe, waiting for the waters of Hellespont to calm down.

Something must have awoken Hero, who had fallen exhausted into the arms of her sweet dream. She went down to the beach and discovered with horror the body of her handsome lover. Her heart broke at seeing the death of the person who had risked his life for love, and she also wanted to die.

After kissing her beloved Leander for the last time, the beautiful Hero threw herself into the sea, where she perished swaying in the waves, the same waves that had separated her from her love.

> *In her bosom plung'd the sword,*
> *All warm and reeking from its slaughter'd lord.*

Ovid

5. PYRAMUS AND THISBE

Forbidden love

Here is another unfortunate story of love that ends in tragedy, the legend of a forbidden love.

There lived in Babylon two youths, *Pyramus* and *Thisbe*, who had the good fortune to be deeply in love and live in houses next to each other and the misfortune to belong to families whose rivalry went back generations. Both the parents of the young man and those of the young woman had categorically forbidden them to see or talk to each other.

The love that united them, however, was too strong for them to obey their families, and taking advantage of the fact that their rooms were next to each other, Pyramus managed to open a hole in the wall through which they could see each other, talk, and even hold hands. But with the passing of time, that was not enough, and they yearned for more intense, longer visits. They then decided to meet at nightfall beneath the mulberry bush that was on the outskirts of the city.

Thisbe was so anxious to see Pyramus that she was the first to arrive at the meeting place. So that time would pass sooner, she started to collect some flowers to make herself a crown so she might be even more beautiful. She had col-

33

lected several when she heard the snapping of a dry branch. Thinking that it must be her young lover, she laughed cheerfully and walked toward the bush when, frightened, she realised in fact it was a fierce lion approaching her, licking its bloody jaw. She screamed, terrified, and took flight. Thisbe's veil fell to the ground, and the lion grabbed it and tore it to bloody shreds.

A little later, Pyramus arrived running, out of breath and hoping that Thisbe wouldn't be annoyed by his delay. But instead of finding his beautiful lover, he found her bloody veil all in shreds. Just seeing this convinced Pyramus that the young woman had been devoured by some wild cat, and struck by despair, he took out his dagger and drove it into his heart.

When Thisbe felt brave enough to go back to the mulberry bush, she found the lifeless body of the lover, holding her bloody veil to his lips. She ran to his side in the hope of finding him still alive, but when she realised that Pyramus had taken his life for love of her, she withdrew the dagger from his heart and plunged it into her own, falling dead beside her lover.

From that tragic day, the fruit of the mulberry, until that moment white, acquired the colour of the blood that was shed from the lovers Thisbe and Pyramus.

> *O Arethusa, peerless nymph! why fear*
> *Such tenderness as mine? Great Dian, why,*
> *Why didst thou hear her prayer?*

Keats

6. ARETHUSA AND ALPHEUS

Scorned love

Arethusa was a beautiful nymph who made up part of the goddess Diana's entourage. On one occasion, overwhelmed by the heat of the burning hot sun, she looked for a cool stream where she could refresh herself. She found the *Alpheus* River and chose a place shaded by some trees, where the calm and crystalline water allowed her to make out a fine, flat sand. Thanks to the branches of the luxuriant trees, she could undress without anyone seeing her naked, and she set about enjoying the refreshing sensation of the cold water against her warm skin.

The river, calm until that moment, rose in waves, and a voice was heard. It was Alpheus, captured by the beauty of the nymph and hoped to make her his wife. But Altheus' precipitous urge terrified Arethusa, who saw how the waves rose and came nearer and nearer to her.

Alpheus begged her not to flee and to attend his courting, but instead of waiting for a reply, he emerged from the water and tried to embrace the nymph, who fled terrorised. He pursued her through valleys and hills, woods and meadows, until Arethusa, exhausted, stopped and pleaded for her goddess to come to her rescue.

The young nymph's supplications found reward, and Diana wrapped her in a thick mist and transformed her into a spring. When Alpheus arrived, he couldn't find the elusive young woman, but fate had it that Zephyr, the East Wind, passed by there, dissipating the mist and leaving the spring visible once more. The old god realised the deception, and turning himself into an impetuous current, he launched himself into the spring. But Diana, who had foreseen such a reaction, opened a gap through which Arethusa escaped, submerging herself in the depths of the underground world of Pluto and Persephone. Nevertheless, a little later she started to rise, and soon she could see the sun once more while flowing out over the meadows of Sicily.

But Alpheus, obsessed with finding and uniting with her, found the gap, through which he plunged to later appear by Arethusa's side, who finally succumbed to his impetuous, stubborn love.

They tell how young Greek women would throw garlands of fresh flowers into the Alpheus River and that those same flowers reappear in the Sicilian spring carried by the current, as if they had been brought by the lover river as proof of his love, that although scorned, was finally reciprocated.

> *My footsteps pave the clouds with fire; the caves*
> *Are filled with my bright presence, and the air*
> *Leaves the green Earth to my embraces bare.*

Shelley

7. IDAS AND MARPESSA

Certain love

Marpessa was the beautiful daughter of *Euenos,* King of Aetolia, and granddaughter to Ares. The sovereign loved his daughter so profoundly that he did not want her to get married. Thus, when Marpessa came of age to wed, the King laid down one condition: he would only give her hand in marriage to someone who could defeat him in a horse race; any suitors who failed to be victorious would be decapitated.

Despite the terrible fate awaiting those who might lose, many young men presented themselves, defying the danger in the hope of marrying the beautiful princess. But Euenos beat them all, since there were no steeds as fast as those that pulled his chariot.

It was not that Marpessa loved any of those young men, but she was saddened by the idea that it was her fault that one head fell after another, and she hoped the day would come when one of them would defeat her father. And it happened that *Idas,* son of Poseidon, having come to Aetolia to attend the risky races, was captured by Marpessa's beauty and decided that she would be his. He also realised that winning against Euenos would be a difficult task, so he asked his father for the fastest chariot he owned. Poseidon, knowing the passion his son felt for the young Marpessa, gifted him with a magical chariot.

36

The race was held, and Idas won by a huge margin. Euenos felt his blood boil at being defeated, a defeat that signified the loss of his beloved daughter. It was well known that the monarch was not a very good loser, as a result of which nobody was surprised when he denied his daughter's hand to Idas, claiming that he had cheated. Thus, Idas took Marpessa, put her in his chariot, and fled. If he couldn't have his beloved princess by fair means, then he would have her by foul.

Euenos left swiftly in pursuit, but his horses still hadn't recovered, and exhausted, they stopped while the two youths escaped happily. Euenos could not bear this repeat failure, and he flung himself into a river where he drowned. From then on, the river was known by the monarch's name.

Unaware of Euenos' sad end, both young lovers congratulated each other on their escape. Marpessa had felt attracted to Idas from the first moment she saw him, and being kidnapped by him was the most exciting thing that had ever happened to her. But, suddenly, Apollo, the most beautiful and handsome god, appeared before them, halting the speedy steeds.

The handsome god had had fun helping in the race, and he had fallen for Marpessa's beauty. He declared his love for her and challenged Idas to a duel to the death. Idas stepped down from the chariot, prepared to die for the love that he felt for Marpessa, but Zeus interrupted, declaring that too many suitors had died already, and it was time for Marpessa to decide who should be her husband.

The beautiful young woman observed her two suitors with great concentration: Apollo was, without any doubt, the more handsome of the two; he was powerful and experienced, but as a god, he was immortal, and that meant she would get old while he would always be just as handsome, and he would abandon her, if he didn't do so before, given his reputation of infidelity. On the other hand, Idas, although not as handsome or powerful, had shown his love, and by being mortal, they could grow old together.

Without considering a moment longer, she extended her arms to Idas, who embraced her in return, and declared that she would prefer to share her life with a mortal who would love her as they grew old together. So it was, the young Marpessa was thought of in ancient times as the prototype of the wise and sensible woman.

> *He loved,*
> *Not in the style of offering small gifts,*
> *With baskets of fresh fruit and bunches of roses,*
> *But with a burning passion.*

Theocritus

8. POLYPHEMUS AND GALATEA

Avenged love

Polyphemus, a cyclops, son of Poseidon and the nymph *Thoosa,* lived in a cave near Mount Etna. The giant owned a splendid flock of fat sheep and woolly lambs, and they were his only companions, since he liked his solitude in the mountains, where he meditated while his flock grazed.

On one occasion, he was sitting on a cliff when he noticed a charming nereid riding her pearl chariot, pulled by two beautiful dolphins. The white, delicate skinned nymph was so beautiful and seemed so fragile, Polyphemus couldn't help falling madly in love with her. He abandoned his flock and went down to the shore to attract her attention, so he could declare his love.

The beautiful nereid was called *Galatea,* and she was the daughter of the god Nereus and Doris. When she saw the cyclops making gestures for her to come closer to the shore. She was curious and approached him.

Polyphemus' heart started to beat faster, and he began talking to her of love. However, since he wasn't used to talking with anyone and he was in such a state of excitement in front of the graceful nymph, Polyphemus started stuttering and stammering, talking by fits and starts, and the more he talked, the more nervous he got and the more mistakes he made.

Galatea.

Galatea observed him with horror; she was paralysed in front of the enormous, frightening cyclops, who said incoherent, meaningless things. Little by little, she started to back away. Polyphemus continued prattling on, trying to make himself understood, when he noticed that the nymph had got back in her chariot and was getting ready to leave. The cyclops wanted to reach her, but when his feet touched the salty water, he stepped back frightened. In his excitement, he had forgotten his destiny, which prevented him from touching the water, due to a punishment imposed by the gods.

While Polyphemus bitterly cursed his invincible aversion to water, Galatea escaped, terrified, from that monstrous, ill-mannered beast. The nymph couldn't remember ever meeting such a creature before in her life. She remembered the beauty of *Acis,* a young shepherd she was in love with. He certainly was handsome and sweet.

The cyclops was sad and disconsolate. He couldn't accept that it was his ill-doing that made her flee from him in such a hurry. From then on, he wandered around as though lost, abandoning his flock, and he spent most of his time looking out to sea from the cliff, hoping to see her again.

One day, Galatea invited Acis to come to the beautiful island where Polyphemus lived. The nereid had already forgotten about the disagreeable meeting, and she devoted all of her attention to the handsome, young man. It fascinated her to listen to his melodious voice when he spoke to her of love, and she thought the lovely island would be an insuperable landscape to be wooed in. They sat beneath the shade of a majestic olive tree, and Acis began his courting.

Polyphemus was wandering by, caught up in his thoughts, when he noticed the couple. His blood boiled with jealousy as he got closer. He could not bear that Galatea was making someone else happy and not him. He picked up a huge boulder he found, and with great fury, he threw it onto the unsuspecting lovers who, so enthralled with each other, hadn't heard the giant approach. The weight of the boulder squashed both youths; Galatea, being immortal, escaped unharmed, but the unfortunate Acis perished. Horrified by the mortal urge of the giant, she demanded an explanation. Polyphemus replied that no man, mortal or immortal, would ever enjoy the love that she had denied him.

And Galatea was never again courted for fear of Polyphemus' jealousy. He lived with the happiness given by his certainty that if Galatea could not be his, at least she wouldn't be anyone else's. Other versions tell, however, how Galatea gave in to the cyclops' desires, moved by the giant's suffering and that she bore him three children: *Galas, Celtus,* and *Illyrius.*

They also tell of the legend that, beneath the boulder where the mutilated body of Acis lay, a spring of blood appeared that later transformed into a spring of crystalline water, which ran to the sea to reunite with Galatea without Polyphemus being able to do anything to stop it.

> *A hunter once in a grove reclined,*
> *To shun the noon's bright eye,*
> *And oft he wooed the wandering wind*
> *To cool his brow with its sigh.*

Moore

9. CEPHALUS AND PROCRIS

Jealous love

This is a sad, beautiful sad legend of love and jealousy, which the ancients used to explain the effect of the sunrays on dew.

This allegory tells the story of *Cephalus*, a hunter, son of *Deion* and *Diomede,* and *Procris,* daughter of King Erecteus of Athens. When both youths met, they were shot by Eros' mischievous arrows. The effect of the arrows was explosive, and they got married immediately. The couple's happiness was envied by all who knew them. They were

41

never apart from each other; they always held hands and exchanged words of love.

The good fortune they shared was ended one day when Cephalus wanted to test his wife's fidelity. He disguised himself as a wealthy foreigner and tried to seduce her with expensive gifts and promises of happiness. At first, Procris rejected him, but finally she conceded to the pleas of her suitor. Cephalus then revealed his identity, and she fled in shame to Crete, where Artemis received and consoled her.

The separation was very hard for both of them, since they were not used to separating for very long periods of time. Both wanted to be together again, but neither of them dared to take the first step: Procris because she was ashamed and Cephalus, hurt and resentful. But one day, Procris couldn't bear it any longer, and she left disguised as a young seductress. She also took two gifts with her made by Artemis: a dog called *Lelaps* and a magical javelin.

Procris seduced Cephalus, and she offered both gifts in return for his love. Cephalus felt flattered and accepted her. When Procris revealed who she was, the young man felt ashamed and asked for his wife's pardon, and they reconciled with each other. Happiness thus returned to rule over the lives of the young couple. Cephalus went more often now to hunt since thanks to Artemis' two gifts, he caught more game when hunting. *Lelaps* was the fastest dog in all of Greece, and the magical javelin never erred once thrown.

Eos, the Aurora, who had been happy to see how the couple split up, couldn't bear to see their reconciliation. She felt terribly jealous seeing so much happiness and decided to split them up again. She went to talk to Procris and told her the real reason her husband spent so much hunting was because he had a lover, a beautiful nymph, with whom he made love in a solitary meadow.

The following day, blinded by jealousy, Procris followed her husband. When he arrived at the solitary meadow and started looking from one side to another, Procris thought he was looking for his lover. Hidden behind a thick bush, she stood on a branch without noticing and produced a dry snapping sound. Hearing it, Cephalus thought it was a wild boar that he had been looking for a long time, and he

Cephalus.

spun around quickly toward where Procris was hiding to attack it. The sun was in his eyes, and its rays blinded him. Realising that her husband was about to throw the javelin, she stepped forward to explain to him what had happened, but the sound of the bush made the hunter throw his lance with such speed that Procris didn't have time to call him.

Even blinded by the sun, the throw of the javelin was as true and effective as always, and it struck the poor Procris' heart. Hearing his wife's groan, he ran in search of her and found her in agony. Fortune had it that before she exhaled her last breath, both of them explained what had happened, and Procris died, thus, at peace with the conviction that her husband's heart was all hers. Some versions tell how Cephalus couldn't bear this new separation, so he threw himself into the sea to reunite with his beloved wife.

> *Beloved, I am the only one that keeps*
> *His identity hidden and if you were to see*
> *My face, I would have to abandon you: the high gods*
> *Unite Love with Faith, and he withdraws himself*
> *From the gaze full of Knowledge.*

Lewis Morris

10. PSYCHE AND CUPID

Love and the soul

This lovely Greco-Roman legend tells of a king who had three extremely beautiful daughters. Although these three were known world-wide for their incomparable splendour, the youngest of the sisters, *Psyche,* was, without a doubt, the most graceful and attractive of them all. Her exquisite looks and charm were such that the kingdom's subjects forgot their devotion to Venus and, instead, adored Psyche, who they praised as their goddess of Beauty.

Offended, the goddess couldn't bear such humiliation, nor witness how her temples remained deserted, while hon-

44

ours were bestowed on the attractive Psyche. She ordered her son Cupid to make the young woman fall in love with the most monstrous being on all Earth, hoping that this would serve as an exemplary punishment. The speedy Cupid set off with his bow and arrows to fulfil Venus' orders. But when he was face to face with Psyche, he couldn't stop himself from falling in love with such a wondrous creature. Since he didn't want to upset his mother, he devised a plan to calm her rage and enjoy Psyche's love at the same time.

The opportunity Cupid was waiting for presented itself when the King consulted an oracle about why his two elder daughters had married, while the youngest, the most beautiful of all, couldn't find a suitor. The oracle, none other than Cupid's voice, ordered the King to dress his daughter in her finest clothes and then leave her high on a hill to be married to a terrible, flying monster endowed with the ferocity of a viper, before whom even almighty Zeus trembled.

The King, in spite of his despair and the moans and laments of the bride's entourage, obeyed the order of the gods and abandoned Psyche on the top of the mountain. There Psyche remained, paralysed with fear, until Zephyr, the East Wind, arrived and lifted her into the air, carrying her flying to a flowering meadow where he deposited her healthy and safe and where she slept peacefully. When she awoke the following morning, Psyche saw that, beyond the perfumed meadow, there seemed to be a palace of gold, silver, and precious stones.

The young woman, her curiosity and admiration both fuelled, approached the palace where some voices encouraged her to go inside. Psyche opened the gold door and excitedly contemplated the most beautiful of palaces; she found luxurious rooms with exquisite carpets, expensive brocade curtains, and rich tapestries. In one of these rooms, she found a gold bath filled with bubbles and warm water, and she set about enjoying a pleasant bath. In this same room, she also found an enormous wardrobe full of beautiful clothes and a comfortable bed. Once she was ready, she went down the stairs, guided by invisible servants, and entered into the main dining room. Night had already fallen, and just one candle illuminated the great room.

Psyche remembered the oracle and thought that the awful monster was waiting for her. However, she heard a sweet voice that asked her to come closer. The young woman obeyed, intoxicated by that voice and the pleasant aroma given off. That was when she felt the smooth touch of his skin, and a shiver of pleasure ran through her body. She realised the voice, perfume, and touch could belong to no monster, and she abandoned herself to the love her mysterious husband offered her.

After a night of passionate love, the husband bid farewell to his young wife, begging her tenderly that, if she loved him, she should never ever try to find out his name or glimpse his face, for otherwise he would have to leave from her side, never to see her again. Psyche promised to solemnly respect her dark husband's wishes, even though she secretly desired to see his face.

Days went by, and Psyche felt happier than ever. She slept during the day to enjoy their love by night. Even so, the hours of solitude that she spent awaiting nightfall made her feel homesick. The ardent husband and lover couldn't refuse his beautiful wife's desire to visit her family. Once again, she was transported by Zephyr, and she arrived home, where she was received by her sisters and father.

Psyche told them everything that had happened and about the love she felt for her mysterious husband. Psyche's sisters were dying of envy, seeing the happiness that made her even more attractive. Although they were married to rich men, they had never known passion like their younger sister had with her husband. To end this good fortune, the sisters instilled doubt into Psyche's heart, inciting her to who discover her husband was, saying that he must be an awful monster if he didn't want to be seen.

When Psyche went back to the palace with her husband, doubt was burning inside her, and that same night, after waiting for him to fall asleep, she took a candle and brought it close to light him up. Instead of finding a frightful monster, she found Cupid, the most beautiful and charming of gods. Stunned by his good looks, she wanted to see him better and went even closer. Unfortunately a drop of boiling wax fell on her divine husband's shoulder. He awoke, shocked and in

46

pain, and reproached Psyche for her lack of confidence. Then as he had sworn, he disappeared.

Psyche went mad with pain and set off in search of him. She travelled throughout all of Greece, but she couldn't find him. In despair, she went to Venus, who, delighted at having the chance to avenge herself personally of the young woman, kept her in her service at the palace. She had locked Cupid up at the top of a tower of the same place as punishment for his disobedience.

Venus told that unhappy youth that if she wanted to regain her son's favours, she would have to overcome some tests. Psyche was swift to accept, without even asking what those tests might be. First the goddess asked her to separate the grain of seven different types of cereals that she herself had mixed in a mountain as tall as she. The young woman completed the task successfully, thanks to the help of some ants who had taken pity on her. Next, she asked her to fetch a bucket of water from the River Styx, famous for being inaccessible. She succeeded though, with the help of an eagle. She also tamed the terrible Cerberus in order to reach Persephone's throne. She had to go to the deepest place in hell to bring Venus the Queen of darkness' secret of beauty. Persephone gave the young woman a chest that contained a lotion. The lotion restored beauty to anyone it was applied to, and only the dark goddess knew its recipe.

When she was about to enter Venus' palace, Psyche thought that if that lotion was truly so effective, she could use a little to erase the signs of suffering that darkened her face. She opened the small chest, which in fact contained the spirit of sleep, and fell into a deep, sweet sleep.

Zephyr ran to Cupid's room and told him everything Psyche had done to regain his love and the young girl's sad fate. Cupid was moved and distressed by the story, and he escaped with the help of his loyal friend. During his time imprisoned in the tower, the handsome god had been languishing for Psyche's love, and when he found her asleep, he wrestled with the evil spirit until he had managed to force it back into the narrow confines of its prison. He woke Psyche with a sweet kiss.

Venus could remain insensitive to their great love no longer, and she blessed their union, forgiving Psyche. It was she herself who took them both and presented them to the council of the gods in Olympus. They willingly accepted for the young wife to drink the nectar and ambrosia to become immortal and thus live an eternal love together with Cupid.

Analysis of the myth

The meaning of this beautiful legend is clear: Psyche is the symbol of the human soul that, through purifying itself of passions and disgraces, is prepared for eternal happiness with Love.

There are aspects in this legend that remind us of fairy tales like "Beauty and the Beast" or "Sleeping Beauty", just as the legend of Pyramus and Thisbe brings "Romeo and Juliet" to mind.

> *Stranger, dreams are very curious*
> *And unaccountable things, and they do not*
> *By any means invariably come true.*
> *There are two gates through which these unsubstantial*
> *fancies proceed;*
> *The one is of horn, and the other ivory. Those*
> *That come through the gate of ivory are fatuous,*
> *But those from the gate of horn*
> *Mean something to those that see them.*

Homer

11. CEYX AND ALCYONE

Envied love

Alcyone, daughter of Aeolus, King of the winds, married *Ceyx,* the handsome son of the morning star and King of

Thessaly. They were made for each other, and their marriage was envied by one and all, even Zeus and Hera. The two gods couldn't bear to see such love and mutual understanding between a couple and decided to end both lovers' happy days.

The opportunity arose when Ceyx left Alcyone to head for Delphi by boat to consult the oracle there. Alcyone said goodbye to her husband with tears in her eyes, since she suffered when he wasn't near her. She stayed on the beach until the little boat had completely disappeared from sight. Then she returned to their palace to pray for her husband's safety. However, the envious Zeus unleashed a fierce storm that shipwrecked Ceyx's boat, causing him and the whole crew to perish in the furious waves.

Alcyone went down to the beach for two days and two nights to wait for her husband's return. On the third night, *Morpheus*, the god of dreams, pitied her anguish and sent a dream warning her that her husband had drowned and telling her to which part of the coast she should go to recover his lifeless body. Alcyone woke up with a scream of terror. She got dressed and went down to the beach, heading to the exact point indicated in her dream in the hope that it had been an illusion. But as soon as she reached the place, she discovered Ceyx's body bobbing in the waves.

Mad with despair, Alcyone plunged into the sea to die alongside her husband, since she didn't want to live without him. The gods, feeling guilty for the pain they had caused, transformed both into kingfishers, the meaning of Alcyone in Greek, that squawk sadly. Thus the gods allowed for the couple to never separate again and to live together forever. They also decreed that they should always live over water.

It was said that these birds built their nests and bred their young on the rough seas and squawked loudly to warn mariners of the threat of a storm, advising them to prepare for strong gales and to quickly seek shelter in a port, if they didn't wish to meet the same fate as Ceyx. To protect the nest and the kingfisher's progeny, Zeus and Hera ordered Aeolus, god of the winds, to calm his children for seven days before and seven days after the winter solstice.

49

Rhœcus beat his breast and groaned aloud,
And cried 'Be pitiful! forgive me yet'
'Alas!' the voice returned, ''t is thou art blind,
Not I unmerciful; I can forgive,
But have no skill to heal thy spirit's eyes;
Only the soul hath power o'er itself.'

Lowell

12. RHOECUS AND THE HAMADRYAD

The punishment of cold-heartedness

One legend tells how a young man called *Rhoecus* took pity on an oak that was about to fall, and he propped it up. In so doing, he saved the life of the hamadryad who lived in the oak. The profoundly grateful nymph revealed all her beauty to him and offered him whatever he wanted. Seduced by her beauty, he asked for her love. The nymph accepted, but she made one condition: that his love be constant and faithful. Rhoecus thought the condition most fair and accepted. Then the nymph ordered him to come one hour before sunset, but Rhoecus said that he would not be able to tell when the hour came exactly. "Don't worry my sweet Rhoecus, I will send you my messenger bee, and she will inform you."

Rhoecus left with his heart full of joy, thinking about the following day when he would be able to see the hamadryad again. The following day, after completing his chores, he went to the city to play a game of darts until the time came to go to see his lover. Rhoecus gradually became absorbed in the changing game; luck was on his side, and he was about to win if he scored a six. Suddenly he heard a buzzing of an insect in his ear. He cleared it away with a slap of his hand, because the noise was distracting him, and he threw the darts. He lost. "It was that insect's fault," he exclaimed with much annoyance, and as soon as he did so, he remembered the hamadryad's words. He looked up towards where the bruised bee was flying and his eyes fixed on the hills behind which the sun was setting. The blood rose to his head, and without uttering a single word to his friends, he departed running.

He reached his love breathless and exhausted, calling her while he clumsily apologised. However, the hamadryad wasn't willing to forgive him, and she told him: "Oh Rhoecus! You will never see me again, neither by day nor by night. I would have happily blessed you with a most perfect, overflowing love that never before has the mortal heart known; but you treated my humble messenger with scorn. You sent it back to me with broken wings." The breeze blew on Rhoecus forehead, "all around him was beauty and charm, but from that night on he was alone in the world". According to other, more dramatic, less poetic versions, Rhoecus lost his sight.

Slow, fugitive beauty, slow your speed,
Forget your fears and turn your glorious head;
You will see a tired lover with the best of desires.

Prior

13. DAPHNE

Mutation of escape

Daphne was a stunning wood nymph and daughter of the Thessalian river god Peneus and the priest-nymph Gea. One day, she was walking in the woods, day-dreaming to her songs, when she bumped into the handsome god Apollo. He was charmed by the attractive nymph's appearance and smiled at her. Shocked, Daphne moved back. Apollo tried to win the young woman's affection by talking to her gently. The handsome god felt a devouring passion for the nymph, and as he talked and smiled at her, his pulse raced with lust. He tried to get closer, but the nymph, discerning the ravenous desire in his gaze, moved back again.

51

Seeing the fear his approach produced and unable to bear waiting a minute longer, Apollo decided to throw himself on her to possess her, the sweet moves of seduction completely forgotten. But the agile nymph was faster than the impulsive god, and she fled flying. The god refused to be beaten and took flight in her pursuit. While flying, he invited her to stop, promising that he wouldn't cause her any harm, rather he would give her infinite pleasure.

Presented with such a promise, the nymph accelerated. Neither Apollo's promises nor entreaties could convince her to stop. However, her strength started to fail her, and terrorised, she realised that her pursuer would eventually catch her. Luckily she found herself near her father's current, and with a final effort, she rushed to find him to beg for his protection. As soon as her feet touched the ground, a strange force petrified her. Her feet turning into roots and her legs into a trunk. And at the precise moment when Apollo landed with his arms open to embrace the elusive nymph, a thick bark had covered her body, and her arms had filled with leaves.

Apollo, having seen the nymph land just seconds before, didn't realise that he was embracing a laurel tree. But then he understood and declared that from that very moment, the laurel would be his favourite tree. He made a crown with leaves from the tree. The tree was thus consecrated to Apollo, and the crown of its bright leaves became the prize received by the greatest poets, musicians, and artists.

> *Emongst these leaues she made a Butterflie,*
> *With excellent deuice and wondrous flight,*
> *Fluttring among the Oliues wantonly,*
> *That seem'd to liue, so like it was in sight:*
> *The veluet nap which on his wings doth lie,*
> *The silken downe with which his backe is dight,*
> *His broad outstretched hornes, his [h]ayrie thies,*
> *His glorious colours, and his glittering eies.*

> Spenser

52

Apollo and Daphne.

14. ARACHNE

Mutation of impudence

It is told how the goddess Athena's somewhat virile taste for war was compensated for by her interest in sewing, an activity which was exclusively feminine at that time. Legend also tells how the goddess was as nimble with the sword as she was with a knitting needle.

In those times, there lived in Lydia, an ancient region of Asia Minor, on the shores of the Aegean Sea, an attractive girl called *Arachne*. The young woman, daughter of Idmon of Colophon, a city reputed for its purple dyes, demonstrated great skill in weaving and sewing. She was also excessively proud and boasted that she was the best weaver, better even than Athena herself, the accepted seamstress of Olympus.

There are two versions from this point. One tells how the goddess accepted the challenge, and Arachne wove a piece of tapestry that depicted the loves of the Olympian gods with such mastery that the goddess couldn't find a single defect. She exploded with rage and first tore apart the tapestry, then turned on the proud Arachne. Arachne was terrorised and preferred hanging herself with a rope than bearing more of Athena's blows. Athena, regretting her actions, turned her into a spider before she hanged.

The other legend tells how a competition was held between them. Arachne chose the kidnapping of Europa and Athena her competition with Poseidon. The competitors worked in silence night and day, while their works of art took shape beneath their skilled fingers. Once they completed their work, they observed both tapestries, and Arachne had to admit defeat. Such a defeat was very humiliating for one as proud as she. It was so unbearable for Arachne, she decided to commit suicide, hanging herself from a tree with a rope. The goddess, though, took pity on her and transformed her into a spider that incessantly wove beautiful webs that sparkled in the sunlight.

For some Greek mythologists, this was the model punishment for all arrogant mortals. Others assert that this legend serves to explain a kind of rivalry between Athenian weaving and that of Lydia. It remains, regardless, a charming legend about the hard-working spider that weaves and spins without rest.

The heart that has truly loved never forgets,
But as truly loves on to the close;
As the sunflower turns on her god when he sets
The same look that she turned when he rose.

Moore

15. CLYTIE

Mutation of fixation

Legend tells how there was a beautiful young women called *Clytie,* who loved Apollo so deeply, she closely watched his daily journey from the moment he left his palace, illuminating the dark sky in the morning, until he returned to the distant seas in the West, dyeing the sky with colours at night. Clytie followed his path with eyes full of love, thinking that, maybe one day, the beautiful, golden god would notice her. But that day never came, and Clytie was languishing for love until the gods, moved by such fervour, decided to transform her into a magnificent plant, the sunflower.

But even as a sunflower, Clytie couldn't forget the object of her love; and now, as an emblem of constancy, she still turns her face toward the brilliant star on its daily journey across the sky.

So close are we to path of the stars
That often, in the pale bright nocturnes,
The distant sounds of their harmony
Reach our ears like dreams.

Moore

16. PHILOMELA AND PROCNE

Mutation of revenge

When *Pandion,* son of *Erichthonios* and King of Athens, was attacked by the Theban king *Labdacus,* he asked for *Tereus'* help. Dazzled by his ally's strength, King Pandion wanted him to become a member of the family, and he offered his eldest daughter *Procne's* hand in marriage.

So it was, Tereus married Procne, and they had a son they called *Itys.* But after a short time, Tereus fell in love with his sister-in-law, *Philomela,* and he wanted her more and more with every passing day. One day, he could no longer bear the idea of not possessing her, and after tricking her, he led her to a palace he owned in the middle of the woods, where he raped her. Once his lust had been satisfied, Tereus feared that Philomela would tell everyone, so he cut off her tongue and imprisoned her in the palace.

Months went by, and Philomela couldn't think how to escape, nor did it occur to her how to let her sister know what her husband had done. But one day, she had a brilliant idea and set to work. Before a year of imprisonment had gone by, Philomela finished a tapestry that told of her kidnapping and rape. During one of the visits she received from her rapist, she tricked him into taking the tapestry to her sister.

When Procne saw her sister's sad story in the tapestry and understood her husband's evil nature, she organised a visit to the palace where her sister was imprisoned and freed her. Reunited once more, they came up with a plan to take their revenge on Tereus. Just at this moment, Itis, Procne and Tereus' little son, walked into the room. Procne realised how much he looked like his father and how much his father loved him. "Only the death of his son would make Tereus suffer." And so, with her very own hands, she killed her son, quartered him, and with her sister's help, cooked one part and roasted another, saving the head.

After a day of hunting, Tereus returned to the palace where Procne received him with pretend happiness and served him dinner. Once he had satisfied his appetite, Tereus realised with surprise that he hadn't seen his son, who was always running around the palace. He asked his wife where he was, and she, indicating the remains of the dinner, said "There he is, there's what you asked for." Immediately after, before Tereus had had time to react, Philomela came in and threw Itis' head at his feet.

Pain and anger seeped into Tereus' veins. He got up with a start, and with a ferocious scream, he ran after his wife and sister-in-law. Although they were faster than he, expecting such a reaction, they were soon lost, because there was only one window at the end of the corridor. When they got to it, they held hands and leapt into the void while imploring the gods to take pity on them. The gods heard their pleas and turned them into birds: Procne turned into a handsome nightingale and Philomela into a graceful swallow. Although some people claim it was the other way round.

As for Tereus, he also was metamorphosed; his head was adorned with crests in the shape of a helmet, and his mouth ended in a beak like a lance: a hoopoe. However, some people say it was a vulture.

> *No nymph of all Oechaloa could compare*
> *For beauteous form with Dryope the fair;*
> *A lake there was, with shelving banks around,*
> *Whose verdant summit fragrant myrtles crown'd.*
> *Those shades, unknowing of the fates, she sought;*
> *And to the Naiads flow'ry garlands brought;*
> *Her smiling babe (a pleasing charge) she prest*
> *Between her arms, and nourish'd at her breast.*

Ovid

17. DRYOPE

Mutation of a mother's love

There are two versions of this myth, with the same tragic end. The first tells the story of a beautiful young woman called *Dryope*. This young princess was King *Baucis'* daughter, and she was so beautiful and intelligent that everyone who knew her was in love with her. Such that, when it was time for her to think about marriage, she received many offers. From among this legion of suitors, the beautiful, wise Dryope chose, after much deliberation, a young, worthy prince called *Andraemon,* who possessed all the charm necessary to capture the young princess' heart.

The young couple lived together happily, and that happiness was crowned the day Dryope knew she was with child. When their son was born, the couple's fortune was at its peak. The young wife took to spending every day with her little baby in her arms, on the banks of a small lake near the palace, where hosts of coloured irises bloomed profusely.

One day, when she was wandering with her son and accompanied by her sister, she saw a beautiful lotus flower. "Look, darling son, what a beautiful flower." Indeed, Amphisus liked the flower and reached out with his little hands to grab it. The young mother laughed, and humouring her son, she picked the flower and gave it to him.

No sooner had she done so then some drops of blood fell from the lotus and stained her white dress. While dumbfounded with shock, she heard a voice that accused her of killing the beautiful *Lotus,* a nymph who, fleeing from the god of darkness, Priapus, had turned herself into a lotus.

Fearing Lotus' and the gods' revenge, Dryope let the lotus fall, and picking herself up, she prepared to escape. Her terror intensified when she realised that she couldn't move: her feet were buried in the ground, and her legs started to transform into a tree's thick bark. With a cry of grief, she gave her son to her sister, who watched her with horror, unaware how to help. In despair, she begged the gods' pardon, but before she could finish her plea, her trembling arms were laden with leaves.

Even her beautiful face, washed in tears, disappeared beneath the bark. She didn't even have time to ask her sister to bring her little boy every day to play in her branches. The ancients say that when the wind blows between the

58

leaves of the tree, the sound made is "the lonely whisper of Dryope for her son".

The tragic transformation of the young woman into a *hamadryad* is told by other writers in the following way: on one occasion, the beautiful Dryope was playing with her friends in a meadow. Apollo, who was enjoying himself watching them, fell in love with her and transformed himself into a tortoise so he could approach her and see her close up. When they saw the animal, they thought they could use it as a ball to play with. They had fun playing catch with it until it hit Dryope, making her lose her balance and fall to the ground. The tortoise turned into a snake and penetrated her. Ashamed at having been possessed by a snake, Dryope asked the gods to transform her into a hamadryad.

> *Their little shed, scarce large enough for two,*
> *Seems, from the ground increas'd, in height and bulk to*
> *grow.*
> *A stately temple shoots within the skies,*
> *The crutches of their cot in columns rise:*
> *The pavement polish'd marble they behold,*
> *The gates with sculpture grac'd, the spires and tiles of gold.*

Ovid

18. PHILEMON AND BAUCIS

Mutation of a reward

This is a legend that Ovid tells in his "Metamorphoses", and it tells how, on one occasion, Zeus came down with Hermes to the Earth. To avoid being recognised, they disguised themselves as travellers. They came to a small town in Phrygia and decided to ask for shelter for the night. Both gods called on several doors, but they remained closed to them. Finally, they came to a small hut, and when they knocked, the door opened.

An old couple called *Philemon* and *Baucis* lived there. Despite their old age and fatigue, they went to great effort to make the hungry travellers feel at home. Philemon decided to kill his only goose to offer them good food. Despite his efforts, the bird managed to escape and hid between Zeus' legs. The excited god took them to the top of a neighbouring hill and showed them the punishment that had been wreaked on those that had refused them hospitality. The frightened old couple saw how the whole town had perished in a terrible flood.

Zeus promised then them anything they wanted as a reward for their hospitality. The old couple made a wise, modest choice and asked that they might remain together for the rest of their days and die together. So the god transformed their house into a magnificent temple, so they could offer their daily prayers at the altar, and disappeared.

After several years, the day arrived when they were both to die, and so, at the doors of the temple, they were each transformed into majestic trees: Philemon into a magnificent oak and Baucis into a murmuring linden. The purpose of this legend was to teach that hospitality is a sacred task, while displaying conjugal faithfulness is the source for eternal happiness.

Philemon and Baucis.

III

THE GREAT MYTHS

Give me, says he (nor thought he ask'd too much),
That with my body whatsoe'er I touch,
Chang'd from the nature which it held of old,
May be converted into yellow gold.

Ovid

1. MIDAS

This King of Phrygia was the son of the great goddess *Ida* and a satyr. Perhaps as a consequence of his paternal inheritance, this sovereign was very fond of pleasure and of luxury from his mother's side. Before proclaiming himself King of Phrygia, he governed over the Phrygians in Bromius, in Macedonia, where he gave proof of his sybaritic taste by planting his famous rose gardens.

It is told how, when he was still a boy, some ants put some grains of wheat between his lips while he was happily asleep in his cradle. This prodigy was interpreted by soothsayers as an omen for great wealth he would have one day.

That day arrived when his gardeners found *Silenus*, the satyr, sleeping off his drunkenness. They took him to

Midas in order for him to be punished. However, when Silenus told him he was Dionysus' mentor and that he'd been distracted and lost track of his group on his way to Boeotia, Midas offered to accompany him until he found the god and the rest of the group. Dionysus, who had been very worried by his mentor's disappearance, wanted to reward the helpful king, offering him anything he wanted. Midas, without stopping to think, replied that he wanted everything he touched to turn into gold. The god accepted, and the greedy king knelt down and kissed his feet in appreciation.

His wish was fulfilled literally, and Midas went back to his palace congratulating himself on his audacious request and entertaining himself by touching flowers that automatically turned into gold. Happy and satisfied with his recently acquired power, he ordered for a sumptuous banquet to celebrate. His happiness slowly diminished as he tried to eat and drink, since everything turned into the precious metal. His irritation realising that he couldn't eat, since he turned everything into gold, transformed into despair after a few days. Surrounded by plenty, Midas was subject to hunger and thirst.

That was when Midas felt rich and poor at the same time. He hated his funereal opulence, which didn't allow him to satisfy his hunger or quench his thirst, and he regretted his greed, realising the stupidity of his wish. It no longer seemed so attractive, the idea of being surrounded by gold, and he just wished for things to go back the way they were. In despair, he sought out Dionysus, who in fact was waiting for him with relish, and throwing himself at his feet once more, he begged to be freed from the inconvenient gift that was making him starve to death.

The god could hardly control his laughter, and he explained that he had to wash in the River Pactolus, near Mount Tmolus. Midas ran and then walked without rest until he found that river and washed himself in it. The sands of the river turned into gold, and still today, you can find small pieces, since it seems that Midas transmitted his powers to the river.

Exhausted and starving, he went to the Phrygian king *Gordius'* palace, since it was nearby. The Phrygian sovereign not only offered him hospitality, but also adopted him, as he had no heir. Some writers claim that Gordius lay with *Cybele*, and together they conceived Midas.

The legend of King Gordius

The kingdom of Phrygia was suffering, at that time, from a series of internal struggles due to the lack of an heir to the throne. Gordius was then a poor farmer heading to the city to consult the oracle of Telmissus. Halfway there, a royal eagle landed on the pole of his ox cart. When he arrived at the oracle's, he was given the order to go to the city and offer sacrifices to Zeus. A little later, he met a young prophetess with whom he fell in love and proposed marriage. The young woman accepted, according to a premonition she had seeing the royal eagle still perched there, and she sat in the cart with him.

Days earlier, the oracle had declared to the kingdom's subjects that a new king would enter the city together with his bride-to-be in an ox cart, upon which a royal eagle would be resting.

When the cart entered the city square, Gordius was unanimously proclaimed the new King of Phrygia. The new sovereign, in gratitude, founded the city of *Gordius,* where he consecrated his cart to Zeus, tying around the pole a knot that was so complicated, the oracle predicted that whoever was capable of undoing it would be emperor and lord of the world. The yoke and the pole were kept at the acropolis by Zeus' priests until, in the sixth century before Christ, *Alexander the Great*, passing through Gordius, took out his sword and cut the 'Gordian knot'.

* * *

Midas proclaimed himself the new king upon Gordius' death, established a cult devoted to Dionysus, and founded the city *Ancyra*. Some years later, the famous competition between *Apollo* and *Marsyas* was celebrated. The King agreed to come by Mount Tmolus where the competition was being held, and he was installed as judge. After listening to one then the other, Midas had the unfortunate and insensitive idea of declaring Marsyas the winner. The insulted god then gave him some awful, frightful donkey's ears.

The King ran to hide ashamedly at his lodgings, refusing to see anyone. After a little while, he decided to hide his ears under a *pileus*, a Phrygian hat, but he realised that he couldn't always wear the hat. He called his hairdresser to his lodgings, making him swear to keep his secret or be sentenced to death. The hairdresser promised him, and upon seeing the sovereign's ears, he could barely stifle a cry of horror. He adroitly apologised and skilfully made him a wig to hide that deformity.

But it was too big a secret to keep to himself. Thus, one day he found a hole near some rushes, and bending down, he wrapped his hands around his mouth so that not one single word would escape and shouted: "King Midas has got donkey's ears!" No sooner had he done so, he filled the hole with sand and left at peace with himself.

Nevertheless, after a few months, some rushes grew right on that spot, and with gusts of wind, they murmured to all who passed near them that impertinent phrase. Soon, the whole kingdom knew the news, and poor Midas became a laughing stock. Unable to bear the sly laughter behind his back, he condemned the hairdresser to death and immediately afterwards drank bull's blood and died.

This is a legend that reveals that both greed and insensitivity have to pay a very high price.

> *My boy* (Icarus), *take care*
> *To wing your course along the middle air;*
> *If low, the surges wet your flagging plumes;*
> *If high, the sun the melting wax consumes:*

Ovid

2. DAEDALUS AND ICARUS

Daedalus' origins are unknown. However, nearly all the versions suggest that he was of the Royal Athenian line. Some writers dare to claim that he belonged to the royal family of Cecropia and that his father was *Eupalamus* and his mother *Alcippe*. What is certain is that Daedalus was a prolific inventor, a prodigious blacksmith, a marvellous architect, and an exceptional sculptor; according the Athenians themselves, he was the great instigator of Attic art.

His apprentice-assistant was his nephew *Talus,* son of his sister, *Polycaste*. The boy demonstrated, from very young, great gifts to become a superb inventor. One day, when he was going by, he found the jaw of a snake, and discovering that he could use it to cut sticks in half, he copied it in metal and created, thus, the saw. Daedalus' jealousy grew day by day, and one day, he could contain himself no longer, since Talus not only invented more things than he, but he also dared to give lessons and advice to his master. So it was that he made him climb to the roof of Athen's temple, on the Acropolis, and he pushed him into the void.

To justify the murder, Daedalus argued that he was certain that his nephew was having an incestuous relationship with his mother. The *Areopagus* assembled to judge him and condemned him to exile.

First, he took refuge in one of the communities of Attica, hence its inhabitants have been called *daedalites* in his memory. Then he set sail for Crete and asked for refuge from King *Minos,* who was delighted to have him at his service, having heard about his skills and talent. And so, Daedalus settled in *Knossos,* where he lived peacefully and enjoyed great privileges. He fell in love with a slave, and they had a son: *Icarus.*

When *Pasiphae,* Minos' wife, gave birth to the *Minotaur*, the King ordered Daedalus to build a cell to imprison the monster. However, Daedalus let his creative spirit flow and constructed a magnificent labyrinth, made up of uncountable passages, entangled rooms that crossed each other ceaselessly, and dead ends, that nobody could get out of due to its complex structure.

Daedalus' quiet, pleasant life ended the day King Minos found out that the inventor had explained to his daughter *Ariadne* how to get out of the labyrinth. As punishment, Daedalus was imprisoned with his son in the same labyrinth; but Pasiphae let them free. However, it was not an easy thing to escape from the island without being seen and in a hurry. The ingenious Athenian thus built a pair of wings for himself and another for his son. He sewed on large feathers with a thread and the smaller ones with wax. Afterwards they helped each other put on the wings.

Before leaving, Daedalus warned his son that he should neither fly to close to the sea, because the water would wet his wings, nor very close to the sky, because the sun would melt the wax. Straight after, they took flight, leaping off a cliff to the Northeast of the island, and vigorously beating their wings, they started to fly. Icarus followed his father. They soon left Crete far behind, and a few hours later, they passed Naxos, Delos, and Paros, to the left, and Lebynthos and Calymne to the right. The fishermen and farmers on these islands marvelled at this spectacle and believed them to be two gods.

Icarus, thrilled by the sensation of flying, suddenly felt himself very powerful, capable of anything, and ignoring his father's advice, he climbed higher and higher, until he was in the direct path of the sun's rays. After feeling the cold of the wind, Icarus appreciated the pleasant warmth of the sun, but soon the rays got stronger, and the wax started to melt. When he noticed, it was already too late, and he started to fall at full speed, until he crashed violently into the sea.

His father, not noticing his absence since he was absorbed in thoughts about his escape, turned his head and, not finding his son, got worried and called for him. His worst fears were confirmed when he made out some feathers on the sea's surface. He circled over the feathers, until a few minutes later his son's corpse emerged. He picked it up and took it to a nearby island, where he buried it. The

Icarus.

island and the surrounding sea have been called *Icaria* ever since, in honour of the daring young boy.

Daedalus resumed his journey and settled in Cumae, near Naples. There he constructed a temple to Apollo and devoted his wings to it. Later, he headed for Sicily, where King Cocalus received him hospitably and converted him into his main architect. He lived there until he died, enjoying great fame, constructing beautiful buildings, and creating new, ingenious contraptions. They say that he also drew up plans for an impregnable city that only needed three or four men for its defence; that he invented the carpenter's brace, the level, and the axe, and that he was the first to exchange rowing boats for sailing ships.

Analysis of the myth

Icarus embodies youth, imprudence, and daring, in contrast to his father, the prototype of the mature, sensible man, and for some he personifies the humanitarian man: the complete artist. This character almost certainly has a historical basis. This myth has inspired artists more than musicians or writers: Icarus' fall inspired Blondel, Rubens, Tintoretto, Rodin, Bruegel Senior; and Daedalus attaching the wings to his son, Donatello, Canova, Saraceni, and Fetti.

Icarus' figure enjoys, however, a great notoriety. It is often used as a literary metaphor, emphasising one of two things: one positive aspect, in that Icarus is presented as an adventurer in search of the absolute, and he falls victim to his own daring, and the other negative aspect in that he represents the man that accepts power imprudently and that, unable to sustain that power, falls with greater force.

The labyrinth originated in Egypt – the first labyrinth was built by Amenembe of the Twelfth Dynasty – and was an underground monument carved in the rock that served generally as the tomb of an important person and protected it at the same time from looting. It would appear that his custom reached the island of Crete, but in contrast to the Egyptian labyrinth, the Cretans built it in the open air, and it had a succession of rooms and corridors mixed together, designed in such a way that it was practically impossible to find the way out. This idea was taken up again by Le Nôtre to create the magnificent gardens of the Palace of Versailles, and later, served as inspiration for other royal gardens. We can also find the labyrinth as a game in amusement parks or as a cinematographic tool in films such as "The Shining" or "Orlando".

> *Thus moaned Attica, oppressed by misfortune;*
> *The evils in his country inflame the heart of brave*
> *Theseus;*
> *His generous spirit resolves to save*
> *Cecrop's great descendants from a temporary tomb.*

> Catullus

3. MINOS AND THE MINOTAUR

Europa, after begetting with Zeus *Minos, Rhadamanthys,* and *Sarpedon*, married *Asterius*, King of Crete. The monarch adopted Europa's three sons, and after his death, Minos succeeded him. Nevertheless, Sarpedon was not in agreement and argued that it would be fairer for them to divide the kingdom into three parts. Minos expelled him from the island for this rebellion and Sarpedon fled to Asia Minor, where he allied with Cilix against the Termilians, conquering them and proclaiming himself king. They say that Zeus gave him the privilege of living for three generations, after which he was succeeded by Lycus, and the kingdom became known as Lycia in his honour.

Another tradition tells how Rhadamanthys also found himself obliged to flee from Crete, and he sought refuge in Boeotia, where he married *Alcmene,* Amphytrion's widow. Nevertheless, his mark was left in Crete through the laws he established, such as the Cretan Code, which he edited.

Minos married *Pasiphae,* Helius' daughter, with whom he had four children: *Androgeus, Glaucus, Ariadne,* and

71

Phaedra. There is an interesting legend about Glaucus, the least well known son of Minos.

The legend of Glaucus

Tradition tells how one day Glaucus was chasing a mouse when he disappeared. No one could find him anywhere, and yet, there was not a corner of the palace or the island left untouched in his search. His father, in despair, consulted an oracle, who told him that "only that which explains the daily change of one of his herd's cows first white, then red, and finally black could help him find and save his son".

Minos asked everybody the answer to such a strange riddle, but nobody knew how to solve it until, one day, a certain *Polyeidos* worked out the answer: "The skin changes like a blackberry ripens." A little later they discovered the body of the little boy drowned in a jar full of honey.

So Minos locked his son and the riddle solver in a room and assured Polyeidos that he wouldn't let him out until he had brought his son back to life. Polyeidos then remembered that *Asclepius* had given him some magical herbs that he rubbed on the boy's body and brought him back to life.

The birth of the Minotaur

Minos dedicated an altar to Poseidon, and after making preparations for a sacrifice, he asked the sea god for a bull to come out of the sea to be sacrificed. The god heard his request, and at that instant, a white bull came out of the sea. The king was so enthralled by its beauty and ferocity that he refrained from sacrificing it. Thus, he sent it to mate with his own herd and sacrificed another bull in its place. From then on, Minos gained Poseidon's animosity, and to take revenge for that offence, the god made Pasiphae fall in love with the white bull.

The monstrous love that the god inspired in the Queen made her, confused by that abnormal passion, seek Daedalus'

72

help. At first Daedalus weighed up his duty to his Queen and his common sense, but in the end he felt sorry for his sovereign's suffering; she was prepared to do anything to satisfy her strange love. After much creative thinking, Daedalus constructed a wooden cow covered in cowhide for Pasiphae to get inside. After a little while, the bull slowly approached and mounted the cow, thus satisfying the Queen's desire.

Nine months later, the queen gave birth to a monster with a man's body and a bull's head that was called the *Minotaur*. Horrified by the birth of such a monstrous bastard, Minos repudiated his wife and tried to hide the truth from his subjects. He made Daedalus construct a place where the minotaur would remain imprisoned and would never be able to leave. The inventor thus constructed the famous labyrinth made up of intricate passageways that interwove endlessly and became dead ends. The Minotaur fed on human flesh, as a result of which, in revenge for the murder of his son Androgeus, Minos demanded from Athens a tribute of seven young men and seven young women that served to feed the monster.

After abandoning his adulterous wife, Minos took several lovers, to the extent that pederasty has been attributed to him. It is told that, to take her revenge for his infidelities, Pasiphae cast a curse on her husband's bed so that poisonous snakes and scorpions would come out of it and kill all his lovers.

Minos' death

When Minos found out that Daedalus had not only helped Theseus escape from the labyrinth, but also had been the creator of the wooden cow that enabled Pasiphae's union with the bull, he imprisoned him with the intention of killing him later. But, they say thanks to Pasiphae, the inventor managed to escape and reach Sicily, where *Cocalus* offered him hospitality.

Minos enlisted an army and started his chase, arriving a little later at Camicus, where Daedalus was hiding. Minos had thought up a trick to guess where the inventor was hiding; he offered a large reward for anyone who could thread a snail's shell, something that only Daedalus would be able to do. Cocalus accepted the challenge and in secret, took it to Daedalus, who, effectively, worked out how to do it. He fixed spider web's thread to the foot of an ant, made a small hole at the tip of the shell, and lured the ant through with some honey he had spread around the hole. At the end of the spider web's thread, he had tied a linen thread, and when the ant came out of the hole, all he had to do was pull the spider web's thread until he succeeded in the task.

Triumphant, he claimed his reward, and then Minos demanded in exchange the immediate restitution of his prisoner. But neither Cocalus nor his daughters, all enchanted with the precious toys the inventor had created, were willing to return Daedalus. With his help, they made a plan to get rid of Minos. They designed a tube that reached where Minos was having a relaxing bath and they poured boiling water down it, which fell onto the Cretan king, scalding him to death.

Cocalus sent the monarch's corpse back to Crete, explaining that Minos had accidentally fallen into a cauldron of boiling water. The disgraced king's followers buried him with all the honours.

Hell's judges

In spite of Minos' tragic existence, his people have always considered him as a wise king and notable legislator.

Just as his brother Rhadamanthys first did, Minos used to converse with Zeus in a sacred cave. From these conversations, the King extracted teachings to manage the affairs of the state and a series of laws. Due to his spirit of justice, he sat on Hell's tribunal, where he performed the role of judge.

The second judge was his brother Rhadamanthys. Europa's second son enjoyed a distinguished reputation for his wisdom and sense of justice. They say he enacted the laws that governed the Cyclades and that he was the author of the famous law of retaliation, "an eye for an eye, a tooth for a tooth". Precisely for this reason, Rhadamanthys was chosen by Zeus to form part of the Court of the Dead in Tartarus. Together with Minos, they took responsibility for souls coming from Asia and Africa.

Aeacus, legendary son of Zeus and *Aegina*, was likewise named a judge of the tribunal, due to his decency and sense of justice. He was especially responsible for judging the dead from Europe.

> *But oh, bird of happy lot and fate,*
> *To whom the god himself granted to be born from her-*
> *self!*
> *Whether it be female, or male, or neither, or both,*
> *Happy she, who enters into no compacts of Venus.*
> *Death is Venus to her; her only pleasure is in death:*
> *That she may be born, she desires previously to die. She*
> *is an offspring to herself, her*
> *Own father and heir, her own nurse, and always a fos-*
> *ter-child to herself. She is herself*
> *Indeed, but not the same, since she is herself, and not*
> *herself, having gained eternal life*
> *By the blessing of death.*

Lactantius

4. THE PHOENIX

This myth is not part of any other legend, but its importance in world culture and its beauty are more than enough reason to include it in this modest collection.

This is the legend of a fabulous bird, a legend whose origins go back to Ancient Egypt and that was honoured by the Greeks and widely described by some of the Ancient writers; the first to speak of it was Herodotus.

The *Phoenix*, it is supposed, came from Ethiopia and is related to the Egyptian's Sun cult. Its size was that of a royal eagle more or less; he possessed a spectacular plumage, with red, blue, purple, and white feathers. They said that its colours, bright and rainbow shades, eclipsed the beauty of the peacock. Its flight was slow and majestic.

Being the only one of its kind and unable to reproduce, it looked for a way to guarantee its survival. The ancients considered it androgynous. It lived for several centuries in the middle of the Arabian Desert, and when it felt its life coming to an end, it made a knot with aromatic plants and wild herbs, which were consumed by sunrays. The Phoenix placed itself in the middle of the pyre that served both as a funeral and resuscitating fire at the same time. From its ashes, an egg was born from which the new Phoenix came out, which hurried to carry the remains of the previous bird to Heliopolis, in Egypt, where the Sun was worshipped and whose incarnation was the Royal Eagle.

An extraordinary longevity was attributed to the Phoenix; Suidas confirmed that it appeared in Heliopolis every 654 years; Plinius said, however, every 450.

It is told that the first Phoenix appeared at the time of Sesostris. According to one theory, the Phoenix assimilates to Mercury (Hermes), and the self-cremation is considered a symbol of Mercury passing the Sun. Birds that accompany the Phoenix on its flight must be the stars that surround the planet.

For the ancients, the Phoenix was a symbol of the soul's immortality or even the year, which renews itself once more after it comes to the end of its time.

Analysis of the myth

The mythical aspect of the Phoenix has lasted from Egyptian religion, in which the dead soul is reborn as a Phoenix, to the Middle Ages, in which it is identified with Christ's resurrection. In Chinese mythology, a fantastic, androgynous bird existed, representing, as such, the incarnation of happiness and supreme harmony.

It didn't go unnoticed by alchemists and esoteric science either. For them, the Phoenix was a symbol that characterised the regeneration of the world, like an allegory of the rising sun. This same tradition is found among Chinese Taoists, who denominated the Phoenix the vermilion bird, a literary term used to designate the red sulphur of mercury. Nowadays, it is a stylistic figure used to denominate people that are unique in their class.

As happened with the myth of the Golden Fleece and the Order of the Golden Fleece, the Hohenzollern created the order of knights with the name of the legendary bird, symbolising the continuity of this imperial family that had given Germany several emperors.

> *When, blinded by Oenopion,*
> *He sought the blacksmith at his forge,*
> *And, climbing up the mountain gorge,*
> *Fixed his blank eyes upon the sun.*

Longfellow

5. ORION

They say that Orion was a handsome, young hunter from Boeotia. The Greeks represented him as a giant with gold armour and a brilliant sword. Some say that he was the son of *Euriale* and Poseidon. There are several legends about his life and death, of which, as always, there are significant variations in the versions.

One of these legends tells how one day Orion was out hunting with his inseparable dog, *Sirius,* in pursuit, when he came across the *Pleiades,* the seven daughters of Atlas and priestesses of the goddess *Zaya.* These young women's beauty, well known by all, made the young hunter burn with passion. When the Pleiades saw the desire in his eyes, they turned and fled. Orion ran after them, trying to catch up, but they were much faster than he.

This didn't tire him out though and, less concerned about the possibility of not seeing them ever again than losing them from sight, Orion ran with all his strength, and little by little he gained on them. They tell how, when the seven young women started to lose their strength and knew themselves to be lost, they pleaded for the help of the gods. Zeus first turned them into white doves that took off in flight before the astonished eyes of Orion who had just stretched out his right arm and touched one of their tunics. When the doves reached a considerable height, Zeus transformed them into stars that formed a constellation. But one of them, *Merope,* was the only one that hadn't married a god. She had married a mortal, *Sisyphus,* with whom she gave birth to *Glaucus,* father of *Bellerophon,* and ashamed of this union, she refused to shine. In fact, in the Pleiades constellation, one of the stars shines less than the other six.

Orion, with his fickle heart, forgot the seven sisters as soon as he met *Merope, Oenopion*, king of Chios' daughter and Dionysus' granddaughter. That same day, the hunter asked for the beautiful young woman's hand to her father, but he imposed the condition that Orion do some heroic task or gesture. Orion was too impatient and impulsive a young man and completely insensitive, and he thought Oenopion was asking too much. Thus he decided that if Merope couldn't be his by honest means, then she would be his by evil ones.

That night, Orion trespassed into Merope's room and forced her to lie with him. The next day, Oenopion, learning of the shameful news, invoked his father to organise it that some satyrs get Orion drunk, and once asleep, they took out his eyes and threw him onto the shores of the sea. Following the oracles indications, blinded Orion walked to the East. Finally he arrived at the Cyclops' cave in Limnos, who took pity on him and led him to the furthest easterly point from where Helios emerged announcing the start of the day. The first rays of the sun infused the empty eye sockets with new eyes which allowed him to see again.

It is said that is when *Eos*, the dawn, fell in love with him. She took him to the island of Delos where they lay together. But Orion set off once more for Chios, because his heart was burning for revenge. The King heard the hunter had come to get his revenge and hid in an underground chamber built by Hephaestus. Unable to find the slightest trail of Oenopion, Orion headed for Crete, and there he met Artemis. They soon made friends, because they shared the passion for hunting.

However, Apollo did not look well on his sister's new friendship and feared that Orion would force himself on her, like he had done with Merope or seduce her like he had Eos. Thus, to avoid any greater evils, Apollo went to talk with Gaea, Mother Earth, and persuaded her to send some monster to kill Orion, under the false accusation that this same man had stated that he would hunt all the creatures on Mother Earth. Gaea sent a giant scorpion, and Orion struggled with it for hours. Seeing himself vanquished, he dove into the sea and swam to Delos, in the hope that Eos would help him.

Seeing his plan had failed, Apollo took his sister to a cliff and, pointing at Orion, told her: "That black spot in the water is the head of the evil *Candaor*, who has just seduced one of your priestesses." Sharp Apollo was not lying since Candaor was the Boeotian nickname for Orion, though, Artemis didn't know it. The goddess took out one of her arrows, drew the bow, and after aiming with care, fired.

Artemis discovered the identity of her victim with horror, and inconsolable at the loss, she led him and his dog *Sirius* to the sky, transforming them into constellations.

Analysis of the myth

The explanations of this myth are related to astrological interpretations. The Greeks believed that Orion walked the skies followed by his faithful dog, *Sirius,* and that with their passing, they made all the other stars flee, paling before his bright light, his golden armour. It is known that when mariners who had lost their way saw the constellation appear or disappear, they would say the giant hunter was opening routes from one island to another. In summer, when it appeared in the East, they would say Orion was falling in love with Eos, and when it appeared at midnight, it was a sign that they should start harvesting. Since Orion remained invisible for part of the year, some people created the myth of his death at the hands of Artemis.

In the same way, there's another legend that explains why Scorpio's constellation is behind Orion's, as if it is eternally pursuing him. It is supposed that, given that Artemis was the virgin goddess and despite the affection she felt for Orion, she refused to sleep with him. He tried to force her, and then she made a terrible, enormous scorpion rise from Chios Hill to kill him.

> *Then I arise; and climbing Heaven's blue dome,*
> *I walk over the mountains and the waves,*
> *Leaving my robe upon the Ocean foam.*
> *My footsteps pave the clouds with fire; the caves*
> *Are filled with my bright presence, and the air*
> *Leaves the green Earth to my embraces bare.*

Shelley

6. AMPHYTRION

Electryon, son of *Perseus* and *Andromeda,* and husband of *Anaxo,* ruled in Mycenae when the sons of King *Pterelaus* arrived reclaiming the throne of the city, which had belonged to their ancestor *Mestor.* Evidently, King Electryon refused to consent to such demands, so the Taphians and Teleboans then seized possession of Electryon's herds. Eight of the King's sons died during the skirmishes, and the only children who survived and escaped were his son *Lycimnius,* the bastard son he had with a Phrygian slave, and *Alcmene.*

The king left to avenge his sons and recover his flocks, leaving his nephew *Amphytrion* as his regent with the promise of giving him Alcmene's hand in marriage should he return victorious. A few days later, Amphytrion was informed that the oxen stolen were now in the king of Elis' hands and that he could get them back by paying an enormous reward. Thinking he could marry Alcmene in this way without any blood being spilt, the regent paid the reward and called Electryon to identify the oxen.

His nephew's actions didn't please the King in the slightest, and he reproached him for accepting such fraud, "What right did you have to pay for something belonging to me?" His anger left Amphytrion speechless, and in an attempt to release his frustration, he threw a mallet at one of the cows, with the bad luck that this same mallet bounced back and hit the King on the head. Even though it was an accidental death, Amphytrion was exiled from Argos by his uncle, *Sthenelus*. But he did not leave alone, since Alcmene, who was deeply in love with him, accompanied him in his exile.

They went to Thebes, where King Creon purified them. Lycimnius, having accompanied the couple, took Amphytrion's sister *Perimede*, as his wife, with whom he had three children: *Aeon, Argus,* and *Melos*. However, Alcmene did not want to lie with Amphytrion until he had avenged her eight brothers.

He organised thus an expedition with King Creon's help and some Athenian, Phoenician, and Argivian contingencies and set off against the Taphians and Teleboans, whom they defeated.

The legend tells that Poseidon had put a golden hair on his son Pterelaus' head, which gave him immortality. However, *Comaetho*, the King's daughter, who was in love with Amphytrion, decided to help him by betraying her father and her land. Knowing her father's secret, she cut his golden hair while he was sleeping, and Pterelaus died at that same instant. Amphytrion, horrified by Comaetho's patricide for him, condemned her to death.

Following the victory, the just Amphytrion delivered the conquered lands to his allies and returned in triumph to consummate his marriage. But he did not know that during his absence, Zeus had chosen Alcmene to be the future mother of his son, who was named as the most glorious in all Greece: *Heracles*. The problem was that Alcmene loved her husband like no other woman had ever loved a man. Zeus knew it, and he didn't want to force her, since he respected her too much. So it was that he adopted Amphytrion's guise, and Hermes, who accompanied him, took on that of *Sosias,* his faithful servant.

After being received with great gaiety by Alcmene, the false Amphytrion told her without sparing any details about his victory over Pterelaus, the Teleboans and Taphians, avenging thus her eight brothers. In fact, that same morning, the real Amphytrion had succeeded in a decisive victory. Since it took three times as long to conceive a hero like Heracles, they needed three times as much time than for any other child. Zeus sent Hermes to order the Moon to move very slowly, Sleep to send all of humanity deeply to sleep so that no one would notice what was happening, and Helios to take a break for a couple of days. After three nights, in which the god eloquently related the victory and crushing defeat of Pterelaus, and in which he also awarded a pot as a souvenir of such a victorious battle, Helios rose and Zeus disappeared, leaving Alcmene pleasantly asleep.

A few hours later, the real Amphytrion arrived, burning with the desire to lie with his wife. However, sleepy Alcmene didn't invite him to the bed with the enthusiasm he'd hoped for, and she reproached him for wanting to tell the story of his deeds. Amphytrion couldn't understand what was happening with his wife, and he left to consult with Teiresias the prophet, who explained to him what had happened.

From this moment there are two versions: one tells how, angered, Amphytrion accused his wife of adultery and tried to burn her alive, but Zeus sent a cloud that put out the pyre, and Amphytrion begged forgiveness from his wife repentant, but he never dared to touch her again; the other tells that from then on, Amphytrion never dared to lie with his wife for fear of provoking divine jealousy. Amphytrion died a few years later in the course of a war against the Minoans.

Analysis of the myth

The myth of this involuntary adultery has inspired several playwrights, who have always referred to Plato's

"Amphytrion". This Latin writer plays with the ambiguity of the intrigue to the point that it is impossible to distinguish between the false and the real Amphytrion or the servant belonging to either. Much later, Moliere retold the story as a comedy. It is said that Louis XIV enjoyed this play, because he identified with Zeus' character and his extra-marital affairs on one hand, and he found similarities between his own royal persona and that of his private life.

Heinrich von Kleist, the German playwright, published his play "Amphytrion" in 1807, writing a loose translation of Moliere's play. Nevertheless, for differentiation, Kleist presents Alcmene as an ideal woman, who feels a very pure, romantic love for a heroic husband and, at the same time, an attractive, sensual woman, tragically and unjustly tricked by the god, and for this same reason, free of guilt.

Giraudoux presented in 1939, coinciding with the start of the Second World War, his work "Amphytrion 38" (referring to the thirty-seven works that had already been written with the same title). The difference between this play and all the others is the message it has, emphasising Alcmene's innocent virtue faced with Zeus' lying tyranny. Giraudoux was hoping to distract the audience at the same time, transmitting a message of resistance to the tyrant's oppression.

Amphytrion has become known mainly for his matrimonial misfortune, the man that despite finding reciprocated love, cannot enjoy his wife's love. He has become as such the symbol of the cuckolded man, even doubly deceived, since it was against his wife's wishes. Just like Saint Joseph, Amphytrion had to accept that his wife had been chosen by the god of men and the gods to be the most glorious mother, to he that was destined to save mankind.

Finally, just as the name Amphytrion has become part of everyday language as host to guests in a household in Spanish, Sosias defines the word to mean a surprising likeness between two brothers or even when somebody is the living incarnation of another.

I felt A secret anguish and, to everyone's ignorance,
I sought out the oracle Pythia; in vain.

Consulting with my parents, nought could I discover;
But terrible were the mysteries pronounced
Against me: it was my fate, Apollo spoke,
To wed my mother, to engender a race
Cursed and dreadful, and ultimately,
To kill my father.

Sophocles

7. OEDIPUS

The Royal Dynasty of Thebes began with Kadmos, Europa's brother and Harmonia's husband, with whom he had four daughters and a son, Polydoros, Laius' grandfather, who married Jocasta, and with him the legend of the tragic ancestral destiny.

They were happily married until the day Laius, concerned about not having an heir, secretly consulted the oracle of Delphi, who revealed to him that, to his misfortune, no heir was a blessing, because the son he would have with Jocasta was destined to kill him and then marry his mother. Horrified, but not brave enough to tell his wife, Laius distanced himself from their marital bed. Jocasta, hurt by being rejected with no single explanation, got him drunk that very night and slept with him. There was nothing the King could do to avoid nine months later their son being born.

As soon as he was born, the monarch grabbed the child, drove nails through his feet, passed a rope through them, and delivered him to a servant to leave on Mount Cithaeron to die. It was there, later, that the babe was taken in by some shepherds who called him *Oedipus,* which means 'swollen feet', and he was presented to the King and Queen of Corinth, *Polybus* and *Periboea,* who, having no children, adopted him with great joy and brought him up as their own child.

Laius, still with the weight of his conscience, breathed calm once more when his servant came back. He had avoided a terrible prophecy coming true. Jocasta, however, wept in silence at the thought of her poor abandoned son, who, without doubt, must have perished from hunger, if he hadn't already been eaten by wild animals.

Time went by, and Oedipus grew up healthy and happy, unaware of his sad past and his tragic destiny. However, one day, Oedipus beat a companion in a free fight, and his riled opponent took revenge by saying that Oedipus was after all just a found child. Curious, Oedipus went to consult the oracle of Delphi, who confirmed the terrible prediction: "*You will kill your father, marry your mother, and bring disgrace on your country.*"

Believing Polybus and Periboea to be his real parents, before he could perpetrate such crimes and bring destruction to those he loved, Oedipus decided never to go back to Corinth and set off in the opposite direction to travel the world.

Nevertheless, on a narrow path between Delphi and Daulis, fate had it that Oedipus met with a lord who, surrounded by servants, blocked his way. The herald approached him and ordered him in a scornful, imperious tone to get out of the way. Oedipus, as the son of kings, was not used to being treated in such a way, and he flatly refused. So it was the herald hit him, and Oedipus, returning the blow, killed him. Given these events, the lord ordered the rest of his servants to attack the stranger, but Oedipus managed to kill them all, including the great lord, who, to cap all misery, was no other than Laius.

The Sphinx

When Oedipus arrived at the gates of Thebes, he found out that *Creon*, the King's brother-in-law, had taken the throne as a regent, because the King had died in an attack. He also knew that at that time the city was living under a reign of terror imposed by the *Sphinx*.

In fact, Laius was heading for a consultation with the oracle to ask how he could free them from the terrible monster that had been sent by the goddess Hera as punishment to the city after Laius had kidnapped the child *Chrysippus*. The sphinx, head and chest of a woman, wings and claws of an eagle, body and legs of a lion, and tail of a snake, had come from the furthest point of Ethiopia and settled on the outskirts of the city. It forbade anyone to leave or enter the city without first answering a riddle. If someone failed to give the correct answer or hesitated in answering, the terrible beast devoured the person without further ado. Nobody had answered the riddle correctly up to then.

It so happened that one of Creon's children had been devoured by the awful monster, and as a consequence, the regent had promised the kingdom and the hand of the widowed Queen to he who solved the Sphinx's riddle. With nothing to lose, since life was meaningless for Oedipus, he headed for the outskirts of the city.

As soon as he approached her, the Sphinx asked him the question, warning that his life depended on the answer:

What is the only being on earth that,
With just one voice, in the morning has four legs,
Two at noon and three at night, and the more
Legs it has, the weaker it is?

Oedipus thought for a few seconds and then with certainty responded to the Sphinx: "This being is man, because the first months of his life, he is too weak to stand up, and he crawls on his hands and knees; when he is adult, he stands upright on two legs; and in old age, he needs the support of a walking stick."

The Sphinx could not bear the humiliation and leapt from Mount Phycium, falling to her death. Oedipus was then proclaimed king and took Jocasta as his wife. Thus the second part of the prophecy came true.

* * *

Years went by and four children were conceived to the happy marriage: *Eteokles, Polyneikes, Antigone,* and *Ismene.* But happiness gave way to tragedy when a terrible plague struck the city of Thebes, causing the death of hundreds of subjects and filling everyone's heart with great terror. The entire city asked Oedipus to liberate them from the awful plague, as he had done with the Sphinx.

86

Oedipus at Colono.

The King sent some messengers to consult the oracle of Delphi, and they returned with the following enigmatic reply: *"The plague will end once Laius' assassin has been expelled."* Ignorant of the fact that it referred to him, Oedipus issued a curse. A little later, *Teiresias,* the seer, arrived in Thebes and requested an audience with the King. He revealed to Oedipus the truth of his origin and reminded him that the man he had killed on the path was none other than his father, Laius.

At first, Oedipus refused to believe it, but at that moment a messenger came and announced the arrival of a letter from the Queen of Corinth. In that letter, the Queen told Oedipus that Polybus had died and that she was free now to tell his the truth about his origin. Oedipus could not believe his ears, but he could not deny the evidence.

Desperate and ashamed, Jocasta ran to her dwellings, and before Oedipus could do anything about it, she hung herself. The sight of his wife and mother dead was too much for Oedipus, and he cut out his eyes. Expelled from Thebes by Creon, with the support of the entire city, he wandered blind and cursed around the world, only with Antigone to accompany him. She was the only one of his children that showed her love and respect. Antigone served him as a guide, comforting him to the end, begging for food and helping him until he died.

Day after day of arduous travel, Oedipus and Antigone arrived as far as Colonnus, in Attica, where Theseus offered him hospitality. But the *Erinyes,* the fratricide avenging deities that lived in a nearby bush, hunted and killed him before taking him to Tartarus to be punished for the involuntary crimes he had been destined to commit.

It is told how Theseus buried his body in the grounds of the Solemnes in Athens, since they said that Oedipus was a confirmation of the Athenian people's victory, and only Antigone grieved him.

The Seven against Thebes

Nevertheless, the misfortune of the *Labdacids* didn't end here. They were so named in memory of their antecedent *Labdacus*.

When Antigone returned to Thebes, upon the death of her father, she found her two brothers disputing the power of the city. In principle, both parties had agreed to rule alternatively, one year each. However, when Eteokles finished his year of legislature, he refused to abandon the throne and expelled his brother Polyneikes from Thebes. The exile marched to Argos, where he persuaded the King, *Adrastus,* to concede his daughter Argeia's hand in marriage to him and to help him defeat his brother.

The King of Argos gathered a huge army together with another five great leaders: *Amphiaraus, Capaneus, Hippomedon, Tydeus,* and *Parthenopaeus,* who, willing to risk everything and conquer or perish in the attempt, left for Thebes. But Thebes was a well-fortified, defended city, and after seven years of siege, they decided that the matter should be settled by duel between the two opposing brothers.

Following a unique fight, in which the hatred both professed for each other cause sparks to issue from their swords, the two brothers died. The city's magistrate decided that the traitors would not be given burial, and they proclaimed a decree that should anyone dare to bury Polyneikes body, they would be buried alive. Creon, who had taken power once more, abandoned the body of the prince where he had fallen on the Theban mountain to be carrion for the vultures.

Antigone

While Creon organised the solemn funeral for Eteokles, Polyneikes, who was forbidden funeral rites for having dared take up arms against his own people, was destined for his soul to never know peace.

However, Antigone, more obedient to divine laws and her fraternal feelings, since she considered it sacred to bury the dead, ignored her sister Ismene's pleas and putting her own life in risk, went to where her brother lay lifeless. She dug a tomb for her brother's remains and without anyone's help, performed the funeral rites. But before she could finish her work she was caught by some guards.

In spite of the fact that she was his niece and his son Haemon's fiancé (although some writers believe he was the son that died in the claws of the Sphinx), Creon condemned her to death. According to Sophocles, when Haemon saw his pleas were in vain, he entered Antigone's cell, and together they perished. She died of asphyxia and he, a second later, committed suicide with his dagger.

According to other authors, Antigone was buried alive in the pantheon of the Labdacids, and Haemon, maddened by pain, committed suicide in front of his father. After which, Eurydice, his mother, committed suicide as well.

Thus Antigone died, ending a life of pain and suffering, although she never betrayed her self-denial and greatness of soul, unequalled in all classical mythology. Ismene, the last of Oedipus' descendents, died from grief, bringing the prophecy to an end.

Analysis of the myth

The myth of Oedipus, the wise, just king who discovered himself to be an incestuous father-killer, both guilty and innocent at the same time, presents destiny's fate, the unavoidable trap that the oracle warns about.

It is true to say that both Oedipus and Antigone are the most represented mythical characters in Western literary history. The Greek tragedians Aeschylus, Sophocles, and Euripides wrote about this drama, defining the characters that Seneca (first century) took up again, although without bringing anything new of special note. For Sophocles, Oedipus was a hero of tragic conscience. In the sixteenth century, a time during which the Renaissance championed a return to classic antiquity, Oedipus came to be consecrated by the theatre, although he lost his tragic force. Corneille or Voltaire excessively complicated the plot with additional elements and failed to entirely communicate the cruelty of the myth.

In 1905, Hugo von Hoffmannsthal wrote a play, "Oedipus and the Sphinx", in which Oedipus was presented as a man in anguish for his error, victim of a sense of guilt in a climate utterly removed from that of the classic antiquity and even mythology. Under Andre Gide's pen (1932), Oedipus became a hero that tries to take the place of a god who causes him anguish. Evidently, Gide neither believed in the hero's guilt or his responsibility for the crimes committed, patricide and incest.

Jean Cocteau offers, in "King Oedipus" (1926) and "The Infernal Machine" (1934), a poetic synthesis of this tragedy, according to which one must liberate oneself from the gods, the real 'infernal machines'.

Nevertheless, the best known reading of the Oedipus myth was without a doubt Sigmund Freud's. In his investigations, he discovered that during the phallic phase of the development of the libido (from three to five years), the male child tends to build up a more intense relationship with the mother, while acquiring extreme aggression against the male he considers his most direct rival, the father. It is from this that the celebrated term 'Oedipal complex' comes.

For her part, Antigone has served as inspiration to Racine, Alfieri, Brecht, and S. Espriu, among others. The political sense is blunted in Racine's works, for whom Antigone is the model of filial, fraternal piety.

In 1580, Garnier contrasted Creon, law and order, with Antigone. Cocteau, Anouilh, and Brecht treat it in similar ways: the contradiction between the human conscience and the law of the state, which is evident in the rise of Fascism and the eruption of the Second World War in all its sharpness and violence. Malraux then declared, "the Resistance is Antigone's 'no' to Creon".

There were tall trees, moreover, that shed their fruit over his head-
Pears, pomegranates, apples, sweet figs and juicy olives,
But whenever the poor creature stretched out his hand to take some,
The wind tossed the branches back again to the clouds.

Homer

8. TANTALUS

Tantalus, King of Lydia or Phrygia, is considered to be the son of Zeus and *Pluto,* daughter of Cronus, and father of *Niobe, Broteas,* and *Pelops.* A multitude of legends are told about this king, of which, in turn there are several versions.

The most accepted one tells how Tantalus, having the privilege of attending Olympian banquets and affected by his good fortune, stole ambrosia and nectar to offer to his mortal friends, transmitting thus the mysteries of the gods' cults as well. However, Tantalus offended the gods with an even greater crime.

It is told how he invited them to a banquet at his palace, and during the same, he served his son as the main dish. Some say that it was because he realised he didn't have enough food and didn't want to offend them with a meagre feast. Others claim that the odd king wanted to test the divining gifts of the gods. The fact of the matter is that he killed, quartered, cooked, and served up his own son, and when all the gods, except for Demeter, who was upset by the disappearance of her daughter and ate the shoulder of the unfortunate son, realised the horrible, sacrilegious crime, they punished Tantalus.

They brought Pelops back to life, and Demeter gave him a marble or gold shoulder in compensation for the one she had eaten. He emigrated to Greece, where he married *Hippodameia, Oenomaus* King of Pisa's daughter. One version tells how, to win the princess' hand, Pelops received help from Poseidon. He offered him his chariot to win the race for which Hippodameia was the prize. Although he lived his life happily, he didn't have much luck with his children, *Atreus* and *Thyestes,* who were well-known for their cruelty. After his death, his shoulder blade was kept in Pisa.

Another version states that Poseidon fell in love with Pelops and took him to his palace, where he named him royal cup-bearer and bed companion, just as Zeus did with Ganymede. After that, he sought refuge in Greece, where he governed over the extensive peninsula of Peloponnesus, that still uses his name.

Tantalus, received an exemplary punishment for his numerous crimes. There are various versions on this point as well: one of them tells how Tantalus was carried to Tartarus, where he was submerged up to the chin in a current of crystalline waters, while he remained thirsty. A branch of succulent fruit hung over his head, however, when he tried to grab the fruit, the branch folded upwards, escaping his hungry mouth. Others say that a great rock was suspended over his head, continuously threatening to squash him, while he was dying of thirst and hunger, surrounded by water and fruit trees, which disappeared every time he tried to reach for them. The punishment given to the impious king becomes the greatest torture: the inability to obtain that which you desire.

This unique myth has given origin, in the Anglo-Saxon language, to the verb 'to tantalise', which means 'to torment', and clearly has its origins in the Latin word 'tantalus'.

> *The years of melancholy,*
> *The miserable years of melancholy,*
> *Passed slowly until arrived*
> *The midnight of terror.*
> *And for the brightness of the streets in flames I saw,*
> *Palaces and temples falling into ruin and decline.*

Lewis Morris

9. ORESTES AND ELEKTRA

The end of a cursed dynasty

There hasn't existed in all of Greek mythology a dynasty that suffered more funereal curses than that of Pelops, son of Tantalus.

A tradition tells how the curse began when Pelops, wanting to marry Hippodameia at any cost, bribed *Myrtilos,* King *Oenomaus* of Pisa's charioteer and son of Hermes. The King had put one condition on conceding his daughter's hand in marriage, that the suitor beat him in a chariot race. Pelops promised the charioteer that he would allow him to spend one night with Hippodameia if, in return, he substituted the wheel axles on the royal chariot for wax ones. Thus did Myrtilos, and during the race, the wax axle broke, and Oenomaus was killed.

After his victory, Pelops not only refused to complete his side of the bargain, but he also threw Myrtilos into the sea, who, prior to drowning, cursed Pelops and all his descendents, known as the *Pelopids*.

Once Amphytrion had been exiled, and after taking power of the Mycenae throne, *Sthenelus* sent for *Atreus* and *Thyestes*, Pelop's twin sons, and installed them in Midea. Upon Eurystheus and Sthenelus' death, an oracle predicted that the new king would be one of the Pelopids. The two brothers, who hated each other with a vengeance, like Eteokles and Polyneikes, fought for the power, thinking up the cruellest of tricks to finish off the other.

Atreus was selected as the new king, and Hermes gave him a golden fleece as a symbol of royalty. But Thyestes seduced *Aerope,* Atreus' wife, to rob the fleece and seize power of the throne. Atreus was warned by Hermes, though, and he exiled his brother. It was only later that he knew about the adultery his wife and despised brother had committed, and then he decided to take his revenge.

Using reconciliation as an excuse, he invited Thyestes to a banquet, with a menu that consisted of his own children, killed by Atreus' own hands. From his renewed exile, Thyestes cursed his brother and all his offspring and planned his revenge. He consulted an oracle, who advised him to have a son with his daughter *Pelopia,* and so he did; but he preferred his daughter not to know it was incest and he raped her during the dark of night, so that she couldn't identify him; however, she could take his sword. From this union Aegisthus was born, once Pelopia had married her uncle Atreus, who was ignorant of the fact she was his niece.

Pelopia gave birth and abandoned the boy together with her rapist's sword; but he was taken in by some shepherds, and they gave him to a goat to feed him. That is how he earned his name, Aegisthus, which means 'goat's strength'. However, Atreus discovered him and brought him up like a son.

Years later, Atreus sent his eldest sons, *Agamemnon* and *Menelaus*, in search of Thyestes. He locked him up in a cell and then ordered Aegisthus to go there at night and kill him in his sleep. However, Thyestes fought his assailant back and disarmed him. Upon contemplating the sword, he recognised Aegisthus as his son and told him the whole story. As a result, Aegishtus killed his uncle, Atreus, and Pelopia, upon learning that she had been raped by her own father, committed suicide.

From then on, Thyestes and Aegisthus ruled together in Mycenae, and calm appeared to fall on the family once more. But relentless destiny had to take its course.

Agamemnon and Menelaus, the *Atrides*, having been exiled to Sparta, recruited an army and expelled the usurpers to the throne with the help of the Spartan king, *Tyndareus*, husband of *Leda*. Agamemnon married one of King Tyndareus' daughters, *Clytemnestra,* and his brother Menelaus the other, *Helen,* whose misfortune it was to cause the Trojan War.

Agamemnon, being the elder of the two brothers, was the new King of Argos and he became one of the most power-ful kings in all of Peloponnesus. He had three daughters with Clytemnestra: *Chrysothemis, Iphigeneia,* and *Elektra,* and one son, *Orestes*.

The new family drama began when, as the result of his sister-in-law's kidnapping, Agamemnon, named leader of the expeditionary forces, found himself forced to perform a prediction, according to which he had to sacrifice the most beautiful of his daughters, Iphigeneia, in return for receiv-ing favourable winds. However, at the last minute, Artemis switched the victim for a deer and took her to Taulis, where she converted her into a priestess, Clytemnestra never forgave her husband.

To take revenge, Leda's daughter took Aegisthus as her lover during her husband's absence in Troy and used him to plot a scheme to assassinate Agamemnon on his return from the Trojan War.

Orestes was only a boy when his father returned from Troy together with *Cassandra,* a prophetess who was destined to never be believed, and the children he had had with her, *Teledamus* and *Pelops.* Clytemnestra and her lover Aegisthus gave them a falsely embracing welcome. Before the promised banquet, they prepared a relaxing bath for Agamemnon. Once he was removed of his arms and armour, they killed him. Cassandra and her two sons were victims to the same fate.

It is told how Elektra saved her brother Orestes from that killing and took him outside the city of Mycenae, to the home of one of her father's ancient tutors; according to another version he was brought up by his uncle, *Strophius,* King of Crissa. There he struck up a proverbial friendship with his cousin *Pylades,* and they became inseparable adventure and playmates. Meanwhile, Elektra meditated on revenge and awaited, taking the abuse, the opportune moment to restore the logical order in the succession to the throne.

One of the legends about Elektra tells how she was engaged to her cousin Castor. Aegisthus, who was little more than a slave to Clytemnestra during the seven years they were on the throne, feared that Elektra, free of ties, might marry and have a son that would assassinate him in revenge for the death of her father. So it was he delivered her to a Mycenean peasant who respected her virginity, and she lived with him a long time, sharing poverty and solitude.

Orestes, once he reached adult age, went to consult the oracle of Delphi to know whether or not he should kill his father's murderers. The reply he received was that if he didn't avenge his father, he would turn into a pariah and be victim of a leprosy that would eat away at his flesh, but if he did he would be tormented by the Erinyes. Orestes decided to avenge his father, and the priestess, in the name of

96

Apollo, gifted him a bow made of horn with which he could repel the attack of the Erinyes.

The following year, he left for Mycenae where, accompanied by Pylades, he visited the tomb of his father Agamemnon. At that very grave he met Elektra pouring out libations in her own and her brother's name. Thus, Orestes told her who he was, and Elektra's heart alit with hope and happiness, and together they plotted their revenge.

To gain access to the palace, Orestes passed himself off as an Aeolian messenger from Daulis and bearer of the sad news that Orestes had died. He said a certain Strophius had the ashes and wished to know what to do with them. Clytemnestra let him pass, and to celebrate the good news signifying the end of their sleepless nights, she sent for Aegisthus, who arrived confident and unarmed. The lovers were still congratulating themselves when Orestes unsheathed his sword and cut off Aegisthus' head. Terrified, Clytemnestra begged her son to have pity. "I shall have the same pity as you had for my father." Upon which utterance, he beheaded her, and she fell beside her lover. Both corpses were buried on the outskirts of the city.

A little later, the Erinyes appeared with their serpent hair, dog heads, and wings of bats, tormenting him to insanity. Not even Apollo's bow could rid Orestes of the three Erinyes. Apollo, still supporting him, advised him to seek refuge in Athens, in the Areopagus, where Athena absolved him of murder. Afterwards, the god purified him in Delphi, and through pity or priesthood, informed him that he would be totally cured if he went to Taulis and took possession of Artemis' statue.

Pylades and Orestes disembarked in Taulis, and as soon as they set foot on the shore, they were taken prisoner and taken to the temple where they were to be sacrificed. That was precisely where Iphigeneia carried out her duties as Artemis' priestess of sacrificing all foreigners that trespassed on her territory. Just at the moment when Iphigeneia was going to sacrifice him, she recognised him as her brother. Then, in order to save him without raising suspicion, she cancelled the sacrifice, claiming she couldn't sacrifice someone who, being guilty of murder, hadn't purified themselves. Afterwards, she took possession of Artemis' statue and fled with them both to Greece, assisted by favourable winds.

Elektra, who had never stopped supporting her brother and had protected him from the anger of the people who reproached him for the double murder, waited for him in Mycenae. But one day, the news arrived that Orestes and Pylades, to whom she was promised, had been sacrificed at Artemis' altar. *Aletes*, Aegisthus and Clytemnestra's eldest son, succeeded to the throne of Mycenae. Elektra then left for the oracle of Delphi to investigate the death of her brother.

She then met Iphigeneia, who confirmed that she had sacrificed the two young men. Elektra, having been sister, mother, and advisor to Orestes, tried in her fury to blind her with a torch. But, at that moment, Orestes and Pylades appeared, and the four returned to Mycenae. Orestes killed the usurper, Aletes, and married *Hermione*, his cousin and only daughter to Menelaus and Helen, with whom he had one son, *Tisamenus*. Elektra married Pylades, and they gave birth to *Medon* and *Strophius*. Iphigeneia died on Megara, although others state that Artemis immortalised her, assimilating her to the goddess Hecate.

Orestes reigned until he reached old age and died of a viper's bite. Once he'd taken revenge, order was restored, and the curse was extinguished.

Analysis of the myth

This family, the Atrides, marked by a cruel, relentless destiny, which took hold in each and every member and forced them to commit all kinds of crimes and feed insatiable hatred, has served as inspiration for a host of writers, from the tragic Greeks and Romans to other artists from all countries and periods. To name some of them: Scarlatti (1714), Gluck (1774), R. Strauss (1908), in the musical sphere; Racine (1674), Voltaire (1750 and 1772), Alfieri (1776), Goethe (1779 and 1787), A. Dumas (1865), Perez Galdos (1901), E. O'Neill (1931), Giraudoux (1937), and

Sartre (1943), in the literary world; and Pasolini and Cacoyannis (1962), in the realms of cinema.

Orestes, pursued by the infernal divinities, the Erinyes, to the day the gods blessed him with peace and serenity, returning in this way peace to the Atrides and ending the curse, represented less of a tragic figure than his sister Elektra. She was represented by Aeschylus as the avenging arm of the gods to punish their father's murderer. Sophocles gives this heroine the power of choice and freedom, exempt from all ultimate fate. From these writers, other authors could only reproduce the tragic destiny of this woman, divided between two inhuman choices.

Richard Strauss, inspired by Holfmannsthal's "Elektra", presented musically Elektra's inner torment, who found herself forced to resort to violence, in spite of the fact her only aspiration was for peace and happiness.

Just as he had done with Oedipus, Sigmund Freud used the myth of Elektra to define a kind of behaviour which he denominated the 'Elektra Complex'. In contrast to the 'Oedipal Complex', the daughter tends to distance herself from the mother and seek union with the father. According to Freud, this occurs when the daughter blames her mother for the loss of the penis, and envying the one her father possesses, she gets closer to him, because he is the one who can give her the penis she lacks.

Iphigeneia has also inspired a great number of writers and composers, mainly in the seventeenth and eighteenth centuries, when those artists took inspiration from Euripides' tragedies, "Iphigeneia in Taulis" and "Iphigeneia in Aulis".

Iphigeneia was considered an example of the sweet, submissive, resigned woman, due to her compliance with her fathers' wishes. Perhaps for this reason, Iphigeneia has not really inspired writers and artists of the twentieth century, a period in which woman rejected the archetypes of the submissive woman, struggled for her independence, and affirmed her freedom of choice.

IV

THE GREAT HEROES

Minerva gave him the mirror
And, sure of victory, sent him to the battlefield;
The hero did as the Queen ordered,
For which his fame was established.

Prior

1. PERSEUS

Abas, King of Argolis, took for his wife *Aglaea,* who gave him twin sons: *Proetus* and *Acrisius,* to whom he bequeathed the kingdom on the condition that they rule alternately. The differences between the brothers, begun in the same womb, became unbearable when Acrisius discovered that his brother had tried to seduce his daughter *Danae.* Since Acrisius refused to hand over the throne at the end of his mandate, Proetus fled to the court of Iobates, King of Lycia, and married his daughter, *Antea.*

After a few months, he returned to Argolis in command of a Lycian army. After a long battle in which neither party vanquished the other, they agreed to divide the kingdom to avoid more bloodshed. The division was decided in the following way: Acrisius was to have Argos, and the rest, that is, Tiryns, Heraeum, and Midea, would go to Proetus.

Once the waters had calmed, Acrisius went to visit the oracle to ask who his successor would be, given that he only had one daughter. The oracle's answer was explosive: "Your successor will be your grandson, who will kill you."

Against his wife's wishes, he imprisoned his daughter Danae in order to prevent the fatal destiny that was in store for him. The poor girl, shut up in a cell with bronze doors and guarded by ferocious dogs, wondered why she had been shut away.

Despite the precautions Acrisius had taken, Zeus, having heard the unfortunate girl's laments, appeared before her in the form of rain of gold and penetrated her. At the end of nine months, and without the king being able to do anything to prevent it, Danae gave birth to a boy called *Perseus*.

Acrisius thought at first that his grandson could well be the son of his own brother; but when he found out that it was Zeus, although he couldn't believe it, for fear of the god's wrath and in order to avoid his fatal destiny, he put his daughter and grandson in a large chest and launched them into the sea.

The large chest floated and miraculously arrived at the island of Seriphus, where an old fisherman, *Dictis*, brought it onto land, opened it, and found them both still alive. The generous man invited them to stay at his humble abode, and he raised Perseus as though he were his son. The boy grew strong and healthy, and Danae, still beautiful, started to be courted by *Polydectes*, the King of the island. However, the monarch was not to the boy's liking, and as a consequence, she kindly rejected him. He wasn't the kind of man to take "no" for an answer though, and he insisted. Perseus, not liking the sovereign, came to his mother's defence, and Polydectes decided to plot a scheme to get rid of him.

Medusa

Then he pretended that he was going to ask to marry *Hippodameia,* the daughter of *Pelops*, and invited Perseus

Medusa.

to the ceremony. Perseus told the King that, since he owned nothing, he couldn't offer any present as a wedding gift.

"If you really want to gift me something, bring me the head of Medusa. That would make me happy."

Perseus gave his word that he would do so, and he readied himself for the journey. When Danae learnt what her son was proposing to do, she begged him not to go, since Perseus didn't know that Medusa was the only mortal and most dangerous of the three Gorgons. Although there was a time when she had been beautiful, she now wore snakes as her hair, and her terrifying look petrified all the misfortunate people who looked her in the eyes. The legend tells that her transformation was a punishment from Athena for having slept with Poseidon in one of her temples.

After learning the terrible Gorgon's story, Perseus felt somewhat afraid, but he had given his word to Polydectes and didn't want to appear a coward. So it was he departed, and on his ,way he met with Athena and Hermes. The goddess had heard about the difficult task the young man was going to face, and being Medusa's self-declared enemy, she offered to help him. Hermes had been sent by Zeus to look out for his son.

First, they headed for the city of Dicterion, in Samos, where the images of the three Gorgons were exhibited. In this way, Perseus learnt what Medusa looked like and how to distinguish her from her immortal sisters, *Euryale* and *Stheno*. Perseus observed with horror that the Gorgons had a frightful appearance: they were covered in dragon scales, and they had tusks like a wild boar, bronze claws, and wings of gold to fly with. Medusa, besides, was different, because she had snakes for hair, enormous eyes, and a hanging tongue between her sharp tusks.

Hermes leant him his *Talaria,* the winged sandals, and Athena lent the *Aegis*, her shield, so polished that it shone intensely. Even thus, for assured success in his task, he still needed Hades' helmet of invisibility, an unbreakable scimitar, and a magical knapsack. All these items were in the custody of the nymphs of the Styx, but the only beings that knew their whereabouts were the three *Graeae,* sisters of the Gorgons.

Before leaving for the land of perpetual darkness, at the foot of Mount Atlas, where the three Graeae lived, Athena gave him a final piece of advice:

"Never look Medusa directly in the eyes. Use my shield as a mirror to look at her reflection."

Perseus arrived when the three Graeae were playing dice. The sisters were decrepit old women who only had one eye and one tooth to share between them. The young man approached surreptitiously and stopped very close to them.

Each time one of them threw the dice, they took out the tooth and eye and passed them to the next in turn. With impeccable timing, Perseus intercepted the eye and tooth and asked them to tell him how to get to the nymphs if they wanted to get their precious eye and tooth back.

With the information they gave him, it wasn't hard for him to reach the nymphs; he collected the helmet, the scimitar, and the knapsack and flew to the west, where he found the Gorgons asleep. Perseus could see that the barren land was full of eroded forms of men and animals that had been petrified by Medusa's gaze. He carefully approached, fixing his attention on the reflection in the shield until he could make out Medusa, the only one not sleeping. Perseus' smell had woken her, and thinking it strange that she could not see anyone, she kept watch left and right. But there was nothing she could do when, with a well-aimed swoop of the scimitar, she was beheaded. *Pegasus*, the winged horse, was released from her body and flew off. Quickly gathering the head and putting it in the magic knapsack without looking at it, Perseus flew off before the two sisters could descend on him.

* * *

Perseus swiftly fled south with his trophy on his back. On his way, drops of still-warm blood fell from Medusa's head. Some fell over the African desert, from which a breed of poisonous reptiles was created; those that fell into the sea created a legion of voracious moray eels. As the sun set, he made certain to pass near the giant Atlas' palace. The giant denied him hospitality, because he was one of Zeus' sons. Perseus, taking offence, showed him Medusa's head, and Atlas turned into a mountain.

Another version, however, tells how, when passing through Africa, Perseus spotted the giant, patiently holding up the sky, and taking pity of such an eternal, weighty punishment, he decided to help him. Since he didn't have the strength to relieve him, he showed him the dead Medusa's head, and before the smile of gratitude could be wiped from the giant's face, Perseus witnessed in amazement the transformation of the Titan into a great mountain. His mighty limbs turned into the cliffs and crags of a sheer mountainside, and his grey hairs became as white as the snow that rests on mountain peaks.

The mountain range that bears the Titan's name inspired this legend; due to the fact its peaks are lost in the clouds, the ancient peoples believed that they supported the entire weight of the celestial vault.

Andromeda's story

When he arrived at the coasts of Ethiopia, Perseus had a strange vision: an extremely beautiful, chained girl was about to be devoured by a monstrous beast of the sea. It was *Andromeda,* daughter of *Cepheus,* Ethiopian king of Joppa, and *Cassiopeia.* Cassiopeia had boasted that her daughter's beauty was greater than all the Nereids together. The sea nymphs were offended by this insult, and they complained to Poseidon, their protector. As punishment, he sent a flood and the sea beast to destroy the kingdom of Joppa. In despair, the King consulted the Oracle of Ammon, who declared that the monster would not go away until Princess Andromeda was sacrificed. Broken-hearted, the King followed the oracle's advice and left his daughter chained to a projecting rock.

The waters started to rise and stir with foam, while the monster, covered in scales, slowly emerged from the deep. Everyone – Andromeda, the royal family, and all their subjects – was so fixed on the monster, they hardly noticed that

Andromeda.

a young man with winged feet launched himself at the neck of the beast, brandishing a scimitar. Just as he had done to Medusa, he decapitated the monster with a single blow.

When Perseus released Andromeda from her chains, their eyes met and love was born between their souls. The royal family, followed by their subjects, hastily arrived a little later. They expressed their gratitude to Perseus for his invaluable assistance and offered him anything he wished for. The young hero did not hesitate for a second and declared that his only desire was to marry Andromeda. Flattered, she asked her parents for their consent.

The wedding was celebrated almost immediately, but it was interrupted by *Phineas*, King Cepheus' nephew and Andromeda's betrothed; although he had been too coward-ly to face the monster, he now staked his claim to Andromeda's hand. The coward Phineas didn't come alone, rather he came accompanied by many armed subjects and threatened to kill Perseus if he did not leave Joppa.

Perseus asked all those that were on his side to stand behind him, and then he took out Medusa's head. Phineas and his two hundred supporters were all turned to stone. The ceremony was resumed, and once concluded, the bride and groom left for Seriphus. Once there, he discovered to his consternation that Polydectes had tried to abuse his mother, who together with the loyal Dictis had taken refuge in a temple.

* * *

Without wasting a moment, Perseus went to Polydectes' palace, where he announced that he had brought the present the King desired. Entertained, not believing for a moment that the young man would have been able to achieve the task, Polydectes let him pass. In the room, Perseus had to bear his insults and sarcastic laughs, and then he took the Gorgon's head out of the knapsack, and everyone was turned to stone. He pronounced Dictis the new King of Seriphus and left the island with his mother and wife.

He returned her shield and gifted the head to Athena, since she had helped him so much. She placed the head on the centre of the shield. Then he returned the winged sandals to Hermes and also gave him the scimitar, knapsack, and helmet to return to the custody of the Styx nymphs. After expressing his gratitude to both gods for their invaluable help, Perseus headed for Argos, since his mother had confessed to him her true story and about the oracle who was guilty for his misfortune.

Perseus thought to assure his grandfather that he felt no bitterness towards him and that, moreover, he did not intend to cause him any harm. But, Acrisius upon hearing the news of his grandson's arrival, fled to Larissa, in Pelasgiotide. Sinister fate had it that Perseus was invited to the city to take part in the funereal games there. When it came to the discus event, Perseus threw his discus with such bad luck that, thanks to a gust of wind and the will of the gods, it struck a spectator. It was none other than Acrisius, who died as a result.

When he discovered his victim's identity, overwhelmed with grief, he buried his grandfather in Athena's temple, and feeling unworthy to rule Argos, he left for Tiryns, where he agreed with *Megapenthes,* son of *Proetus,* to swap his kingdom for Argos.

Perseus reigned for many years, with great wisdom, together with Andromeda, with whom he had several children, among whom were *Sthenelus* and *Electryon.* The legends tell how, after their deaths, Perseus and Andromeda were placed in the skies, becoming part of the northern constellations, near those of Cepheus, Cassiopeia, and Pegasus.

Analysis of the myth

The myth of Perseus symbolises the courage and audacity of Greek man, fundamental characteristics in the sea expeditions. The three Gorgons came to symbolise the dangers nature causes to people's progress. Some writers focus on the supreme ideal of Greek morality 'to know yourself', absolutely essential for inner balance, to claim that upon seeing Medusa's head, people become aware of their negative side. It then symbolises the discovery of our own guilt, which could paralyse us. At the same time, though, Medusa's head exorcises evil spirits. Consequently, Medusa appears in art, represented in warrior's breast-plates, and also figures in talismans against the evil eye.

> *First of all, to kill the Chimera,*
> *An invincible monster, inhuman,*
> *But divine in origin. Its front part was a lion,*
> *Its rear a snake's tail, in between a goat.*
> *She breathed deadly rage, in searing fire.*

Homer

2. BELLEROPHON

Bellerophon, son of *Glaucus* and grandson of *Sisyphus,* King of Corinth, was a strong, bold young man who had fallen into disgrace after accidentally killing his brother when they were both hunting in the woods. He decided to go to Tiryns to ask King *Proetus* to purify him for the involuntary manslaughter. He hadn't spent long in the palace when *Anthea,* Proetus' wife, tried to seduce him, having fallen in love with him. The young prince rejected her, and she accused him of trying to rape her in her indignation. Proetus believed his wife, but since he was a guest, he didn't dare to kill him himself, due to the laws of hospitality. As a result, he wrote a sealed letter and asked Bellerophon to take it to his father-in-law, *Iobates,* King of Lycia.

He didn't know what the letter was about when he arrived, and he delivered it when he got to Iobates' court. When the monarch read his son-in-law's missive, he was stunned.

It said: *"The carrier of this letter must die. He tried to rape your daughter Anthea."*

Nevertheless, Iobates also felt reluctant to kill a royal guest, and then he remembered having heard talk of a ferocious monster that was terrorising the southern regions of his kingdom. It was called *Chimera*, and it was the offspring of the union of *Echidna* and *Typhon*. It had three heads: one of a lion, another of a goat, and one of a dragon at the end of its tail. It breathed fire and devoured any living being that crossed its path.

Iobates gave Bellerophon the task of killing the Chimera, supporting his request with his fear for the security of his people. Although Bellerophon had heard of several gallant men who had tried to kill the monster never to return, he decided to help the King, because after witnessing the beauty of *Philonoe*, Iobates' daughter, he had fallen in love with her and wanted to marry her.

Pegasus and Chimera

On his way to the southern regions, he met the goddess Athena who had decided to help him in such a difficult task. To do so, she gave him a golden bridle to control *Pegasus*, the winged horse, so that he could defeat Chimera. Bellerophon knew that Pegasus flew down to earth occasionally to drink the fresh waters of the Hippocrene. The legend tells that the crystalline waters of this spring had burst forth when the horse touched the earth for the first time. Pegasus, born from Medusa's blood, was gifted with immortality and an incredible speed.

He had to wait several days until Pegasus appeared flying and descended to the spring where he settled to drink. He jumped just at the right moment onto the white steed, but the horse reacted violently and tried to unseat him. Finally, Bellerophon managed to put the golden bridle between his teeth, and Pegasus immediately became docile and mild.

When he was ready and felt secure, he left in search of the fearful Chimera, which had already given birth to the lion of Nemea and the Sphinx. A ferocious battle then broke out. Bellerophon could avoid the fire breath of the monster thanks to the winged horse's remarkable speed. He struck it with arrow after arrow, until finally, he pierced the lion head's mouth with a lance that ended in a lead tip. The burning breath melted the lead, and it flowed in drops down its throat, burning all the organs of the beast and killing it.

* * *

Bellerophon returned triumphantly to Iobates' court, but he, far from rewarding him, seemed vexed and entrusted him with another mission: to fight the savage Solimo tribe, allies of the Amazons. He emerged victorious once more, thanks to Pegasus. He flew over their heads, out of range of their arrows, and dropped huge rocks on them. Then, Iobates sent him to face the attack of a group of depraved pirates. On his return from his triumphant battle, Bellerophon was attacked in an ambush. The King, tired of waiting for him to die on one of his missions, had decided to murder him.

However, the young hero managed to escape his assailants and returned to the palace without so much as a scratch. That was when Iobates realised that the young prince was protected by the gods and that his son-in-law must be confused or his daughter lying. So he received him with the honours befitting a hero of his class and happily conceded his daughter Philonoe's hand in marriage.

The success of his deeds and the public recognition must have gone to his head. Full of pride and arrogance, Bellerophon mounted Pegasus at one stage and tried to fly to Olympus, since he wanted to prove the existence of the gods and try to gain immortality. Faced with such audacity, Zeus launched a lightning bolt that startled Pegasus, throwing off his rider into the depths of the earth.

For some mythologists, this legend is an allegory of the Sun (Bellerophon) and the Darkness (Chimera), i.e., the Sun rides the skies on the white clouds (Pegasus), killing Darkness (Chimera).

Jason gripped the shining wool exultant
The last of his tasks, and his envied pride.
The fleece ripped slowly from the crisp skeleton.

Horace

3. JASON

Jason was still a boy when his father, *Aeson,* King of Iolcus, was ousted from the throne by his brother *Pelias*. His mother, *Alcymedes*, feared for her young son's life, and placed him in the centaur *Chiron's* care. The wise centaur had already raised other heroes, such as Asclepius, Achilles, and Aeneas. The years went by, and Jason grew tall, good-looking, and strong. Chiron trained him wisely, and the young man became the most astute and talented of all his students. When the centaur felt the time was right, he revealed the young prince's origin to him and how Pelias had expelled his parents from his kingdom. Jason swore then that his uncle would pay dearly for it and his parents avenged.

He left Mount Pelion, where he had grown up under the watchful eye of his tutor, but not without thanking him for his classes and dedication. Chiron gifted him with some golden sandals and a sword as souvenirs.

On his way to Iolcus, he found a river on the banks of which he came across a poor old woman who didn't dare cross, because of the strong current. Good-natured and eager to help people, Jason offered to help her across the river. The old woman accepted his help, and the young prince carried her on his back and prepared to cross the river. It was the start of spring, and the current of water was cold and fast-flowing. After much effort, out of breath and about to lose his balance, Jason reached the other side and with care, set the old woman on the ground. Turning around, he realised that he had lost one of his sandals to the current. When he raised his head, he was shocked to see that the old woman had turned into a tall, proud goddess, accompanied by a beautiful peacock. She was none other than the goddess Hera, who, as a reward for helping her, promised him her protection.

Upon treading on his birth city's soil, Jason noticed that something unusual was happening. He had arrived for the celebration of a festival in honour of the god Poseidon. He made his way through the crowd and finally arrived at the place where Pelias was offering different sacrifices. A while back, Pelias had consulted an oracle and been told: *"Beware he who wears only one sandal."* He didn't understand what that oracle meant until, halfway through a sacrifice, he raised his eyes and saw Jason wearing only one sandal. He observed him with panic and then ordered his guards to arrest him for interrogation.

When Jason revealed his identity and demanded that the usurped throne be returned, Pelias went pale with anger and fear. He would have happily ordered him to be killed, but *Pheres,* King of Pherae, and Amythaon, King of Pylos, both Jason's uncles and present for the festivals, prevented him. Pelias was in no mood to cede his throne so easily, though. Awaiting a plan to get rid of his nephew, he hid his displeasure and threw a banquet.

The legend of the Golden Fleece

During the banquet several songs were sung about the great deeds of heroes like Bellerophon and Perseus. Pelias then asked his nephew what deeds he had performed. The usurper king expressed his surprise at the astonished boy's negative response, saying he would have expected a young man of his talent to have performed some feat. He was certain, nevertheless, that he would manage something heroic as soon as he set himself to it. As he talked, he encouraged the young man to drink. And then the musicians recounted the story of the *Golden Fleece.*

They told the story of the famous ram with golden wool. It was an intelligent animal, with the gift of flight as well. *Phrixus* and *Helle*, children of Nephele and Athamas, rode him to escape from the mistreatment they were receiving from *Ino*, their stepmother. The ram had been sent by Zeus and had carried the brother and sister to Colchis, where *Aeetes* reigned. The ram flew over land and sea; the young girl, Helle, frightened by the waves that roared below, had an attack of vertigo, lost her balance, and fell into a region of the sea that since then has been known as Hellespont. Phrixus arrived safe and sound and sacrificed the ram,

Jason.

hanging the Golden Fleece on a tree in gratitude to Zeus. The poets sang how the Golden Fleece became a talisman of prosperity and power for the god of gods.

Pelias suggested that it was a shame no one dared to go to Ares' forest to look for the fleece. Feeling courageous, partly because of the wine, Jason declared he would go for that fleece, thinking he could demonstrate his bravery to his uncle by doing so and earn his respect like all those heroes had done. And Pelias slyly congratulated himself on how his nephew was stupid enough to fall into this trap, from which, he hoped, he would never return.

The Argonauts

The first thing he did was visit Hera's temple in Dodona and offer her a sacrifice, so she would protect him on his voyage. Hera's oracle, a talking oak tree, ordered him to build a boat from the wood of the pine tree on Mount Pelion and to take one of its powerful branches to sculpt a head that should go on its prow. When Jason finished sculpting the head, it spoke to him, advising him to ask *Argos*, the thespian, to make him a boat of fifty oars.

Jason did as he was advised, and the boat was called the *Argo* (meaning 'swift navigator') in gratitude to the Thespian Argos for his work. Word spread quickly of Jason's intentions, and a crew soon formed named the '*Argonauts*'. Not all mythologists are in agreement when it comes to naming the fifty Argonauts, but we can be certain that all of them were the bravest men in Greece and that among them were:

Acastus: King Pelias' son
*Admetus:*Pherae's prince
Amphiaraus: the Argive seer
Ancaeus: Poseidon's son
Argos of Thespia: the Argo's builder
Ascalaphus: the Orchomenan, son of Ares
Asterius: son of Cometes, a Pelopian
Atalanta of Calydonia: the virgin huntress

Calais and Zetes: winged sons of Boreas
Echion: son of Hermes, the herald
Euphemus: of Taenarum, the swimmer
Castor and Polydeuces: the dioscuri
Phanus: the Cretan son of Dionysus
Heracles: of Tiryns, and his squire *Hylas*, the Dryopian
Idas: son of Aphareus of Messene
Iphitus: brother of King Eurystheus of Mycenae
Idmon: the Argive, Apollo's son
Lynceus: the look-out man, brother of Idas
Orpheus: the Thracian poet
Polyphemus: the Arcadian
Tiphys: of Boeotian Siphae, the helmsman
Butes: of Athens, the bee-keeper
Augias: son of King Phorbas of Elis
Canthus: the Euboean

To speed up his voyage, Hera prohibited Aeolus from creating any storm that might harm them. Thanks to Apollonius of Rhodes' narrative, we can learn the route these veteran Argonauts took. First they arrived at *the island of Limnos*. It had been a year since the men of Limnos had rejected their women, under the pretext that they smelt awful, and turned the Thracian girls they had kidnapped into their concubines. The stink was the result of punishment dealt by Aphrodite for not having received sufficient worship. In revenge, the Lemnian women had killed everyone, old and young, with the exception of the King *Thoas,* whose daughter, *Hypsipyle,* had saved him in secret, helping him escape in a boat. The princess was, from that moment, the Queen of Limnos.

When the *Argo* approached the coasts of that island, the Lemnians donned the armour of their dead husbands and prepared to attack them, believing them to be the Thracians coming to revenge the death of the concubines. Echion was the first to disembark, and performing his role as herald, he calmed them down. Then Hypsipyle summoned a council; they decided, on principle, to offer them food and drink, but not to let them into the city. *Polyxo,* Hypsipyle's old nanny, argued though, that if they allowed the men to come in and they slept with them, they would be able to raise a new, sturdy line of men, since to not do so would lead to the extinction of the people. The old woman's wisdom surprised the Lemnians, but they accepted her advice gratefully.

Hypsipyle, to avoid suspicion, told Jason that the men of the city had been expelled for mistreating them. The Queen offered her bed to Jason, who accepted, and together they bore twins: *Euneus* and *Nebrophonus*. The young queen, having fallen in love with Jason, pleaded him to delay his departure for the good of her subjects, greater in number than the Argonauts. Later, she offered him her throne, but he refused it. And if it hadn't been for Heracles, the only man to stay to look after the *Argo*, who went to call his companions, urging them to come back to continue on the voyage, they surely would never have left for Colchis.

The following stop was *the Island of Samothrace,* where, following Orpheus' advice, they began the Elysian Mysteries. They then crossed the Straits of Hellespont at night, since *Laomedon*, the King of Troy, guarded the entrance and let no Greek boat pass; thus it was that they crossed swiftly, hidden in the dark and keeping themselves near the Thracian coast.

Onwards, they disembarked on the coasts of *the Island of Cyzicus,* country of the Doliones. Cyzicus, the King of the island, welcomed them with full honours and invited them to his wedding with *Clite*, of Percote, city of Phrygia. However, after abandoning the island to travel north-eastwards, a sudden storm blew them again onto the southern coasts of Marmara. They were attacked by well trained warriors as soon as they disembarked from the boat. They only realised that it was King Cyzicus and his subjects after defeating them, with the King lying dead at Jason's feet. It would appear the monarch had taken them for pirates.

Clite, maddened by her grief, committed suicide, and the nymphs of the copse cried so much, their tears created the spring that now goes by her name. Jason and the Argonauts held funeral games in memory of King Cyzicus, after which they set off for the Bosporus.

The *Argo*'s next stop was on the coast of *Mysia*, where they stopped to rest. According to a vague legend, Heracles challenged the Argonauts to a rowing competition, which he won by just one second; just when Jason, the only Argonaut still rowing, fainted from exhaustion, Heracles' oar snapped in two. Heracles ordered his squire Hylas to bring him fresh water while he built a new oar from the trunk of a fir tree that he had just pulled up. An hour went by when he still hadn't returned, so Heracles asked Polyphemus to go to look for him. Polyphemus came back saying that he had found his pitcher next to a spring, but no trace of Hylas. Heracles then went in search himself, with Polyphemus' help, since he felt guilty for his disappearance.

What happened was, when Hylas leant over the spring to collect water, the nymphs that lived there fell in love with him and persuaded him to keep them company at their aquatic home. He was never seen again. However, Heracles and Polyphemus refused to leave the island without him. Jason ordered the *Argo* to leave without them, arguing that they could not delay any longer. Several of the Argonauts accused him of abandoning them to fate on Mysia, but Calais and Zetes, sons of the Boreas, backed Jason up, and that was why, according to the legend, Heracles later killed them with arrows on the island of Thynias. Meanwhile, Polyphemus set up home near to Pegae, where he founded the city of *Cius*. He reigned there until he was assassinated by Kalybs, one of the peoples of the Pont.

On its long voyage, the *Argo* made a brief stop in the country of the Bebryces, ruled by *Amycus,* Poseidon's son. This King had the custom of boxing with foreigners who passed through his kingdom. Amycus was an excellent boxer who had never known defeat, and when the Argonauts arrived, he refused to offer them hospitality unless one of them met him in the ring. Polydeuces, Olympic boxing champion, volunteered.

Amycus not only had the advantage in weight and muscular build, but furthermore, his gloves were studded with bronze spurs. Against all the odds, Polydeuces won; he knew how to dodge the attacks and guess his opponent's weak points. He knocked him out with such a powerful blow, he broke his temple bones, and he died instantaneously. With the death of their sovereign, the Bebrycians took up arms, but the Argonauts easily defeated them. To placate Poseidon for the death of his son, Jason sacrificed twenty bulls, after which they left for Thrace.

They arrived at *Salmydessus*, in East Thrace, where *Phineus*, son of Agenor, ruled. This King had married *Cleopatra*, Boreas' daughter, with whom he had had two sons, *Plexippus* and *Pandion*. Years later, Phineus fell in love with and married *Idea*, rejecting Cleopatra. This Scythian princess, jealous of her stepsons, accused them of trying to rape her. As punishment, Phineus tore out their eyes and imprisoned them. A little later, the gods tore out his eyes for abusing his prophetic gifts; specifically, to reveal the path back to Greece. Moreover, he suffered the torment of the *Harpies* – half woman, half bird – who plagued him night and day, taking his food or soiling it, never letting him eat in peace.

When Jason asked for his help to reach the Golden Fleece, Phineus told him he would only do so on one condition: that they freed him from the Harpies. His brothers-in-law, Calais and Zetes, agreed, provided that their nephews were released and their privileges restored, just like Cleopatra, and Idea sent back to her land. They held a banquet and waited for the Harpies to descend. As soon as they arrived, the sons of Boreas launched themselves at them, brandishing their swords. The Harpies fled, and they flew in pursuit, since, as sons of Boreas, they were gifted with wings. They chased them to *the Strophades Islands*, where they promised to return to their cave on Dicte, Crete, never to come back again.

When Phineus finally found himself released from the unbearable pestering of the Harpies, he kept his word and first released his sons, asking for their forgiveness, as he did with his first wife, and he expelled the deceitful Idea. Then, he explained to Jason how to sail the Bosporus to reach Colchis and avoid all the dangers that could threaten their voyage. In particular, he spoke of the danger of *the Symplegades rocks,* jealously guarding the entrance of the

Jason and Medea.

Bosporus, covered in a thick cloak of mist, in such a way that, when a boat approached, they came together and smashed the vessel to pieces.

Following Phineus' advice, Jason released a dove. The rocks smashed against each other as the bird passed, ripping the feathers from its tail. Taking advantage of the repositioning of the rocks, the *Argo* swiftly passed between them. As told by the prophecies, when a boat passed unharmed between them, they would lose their power, and the rocks returned to their position, where they remained immobile.

Another of the dangers threatening the Argonauts, near the small isle of Ares, was a flock of bronze birds that dove on them with their sharp feathers, wounding them badly. Following Phineus' advice, they put on their helmets, banging their swords against their shields, while screaming with all their might. The birds fled from the unbearable thunderous noise and never appeared again.

Before arriving at the coasts of Colchis, the *Argo* made several more stops. Following the south coast, they stopped at the isle of Mariandyni, where King Lycus ruled. Idmon, the seer, died on this isle, attacked by a wild boar, and later, Tiphys, the helmsman, died from a strange illness. Due to the loss of men over the voyage, the brothers, *Deileon, Autolycus,* and *Phlogius* of Tricca, were recruited. They were brave young men who had already helped Heracles. The *Argo* also passed through the land of the Amazons and the Kalybs.

Finally, they disembarked on the coast of Pont, in the kingdom of Colchis, and they headed to King *Aeetes'* palace, in the city of *Aea*. They requested audience with the King, and when he received them, Jason explained the reason for his visit. The old King was not willing to give them the Golden Fleece for nothing though. However, and to avoid bloodshed, having heard of Jason and the Argonaut's deeds, he proposed a deal to the hero.

Jason's good heart and ingenuity contrasted with Aeetes' treachery. Aeetes was the member of a family involved in magic and the dark powers. The treaty consisted in his giving the Golden Fleece, provided that Jason yoked the two bronze-hoofed wild bulls that breathed fire, both Hephaestus' creations, and worked the Fields of Ares, a rocky land, until forming furrows to sow with dragon's teeth.

While Jason listened in stunned silence to the deal the wicked King was offering him, wondering whether he was up to succeeding in so many trials, *Medea*, daughter to King Aeetes and his wife *Idyia*, observed the scene. Medea was a beautiful, young sorceress, priestess to the dark Hecate, the great goddess of magic. When the young witch saw Jason, she fell in love with him with such a passion, she decided to betray her father and help him.

When Jason was returning to the *Argo* to consult the wooden head about the best way to proceed, he met Medea. She was waiting for him on the beach. The young woman told him that she would help him in return for his marrying her and always being faithful. Since Jason was promised to no one and Medea seemed intelligent, as well as beautiful, it did not seem a bad deal to him given that, thanks to her, he would succeed in obtaining the prized Golden Fleece. Jason accepted, and Medea gave him a cream she had prepared herself with blood-red, double-sized Caucas saffron, which would protect him from the bulls' burning breath. She also gave him a stone he had to throw once he had sown the dragon's teeth, which, Medea warned him, would sprout into warriors. The young sorceress wished him luck and bid farewell with a kiss.

The following day, Jason bathed his body, lance, and shield in the magic cream, thanks to which he was able to avoid burning to death, and before the admiring eyes of Aeetes, he managed to yoke the two beasts and plough the sacred field all that day. At nightfall, he sowed the teeth, from which, as Medea had explained to him, a legion of armoured giants sprouted. He then threw the stone, which caused a battle between them. Finally, he killed the survivors.

When Jason claimed his reward, since he had kept his side of the deal, the King roundly refused and threatened to set fire to the *Argo*, killing the entire crew. Jason, expecting such a reaction, pretended to accept defeat and left. Then, guided by Medea, he arrived at the sacred wood, where he found the Golden Fleece guarded by the immortal dragon of one thousand rings. The frightening dragon was bigger than the *Argo* and had been born from the blood of the monster Typhon.

Medea gave Jason some freshly cut juniper branches from which spilled a narcotic. While she calmed the monster with words of magic, the hero sprinkled drops of the soporific on the beast's eyelids. Once the dragon had fallen into a deep sleep, Jason lifted the fleece off the tree, and they fled together to the *Argo*. Ares' priests sounded the alarm, and the Colchians attacked the Argonauts, wounding Iphitus, Meleager, Argos, Atalanta, and Jason. However, all of them, even the wounded, were able to board the *Argo* and take flight. Medea was able to heal all except Iphitus, who died.

King Aeetes boarded his fastest ship, and they set off in pursuit of the Greeks. The Colchian ship got dangerously close. Medea saw that, unless she did something to delay her father's boat, the Argo would soon be boarded. She murdered her half brother, Apsyrtus, having brought him with her, with her own hands, and cut his body into pieces, which she threw one by one over the side. The cruel strategy forced the inconsolable Aeetes to stop to gather together all the pieces of his beloved son for his later funeral ceremony, such that he had to concede defeat and lose all hope of recapturing his perverse daughter and the prized fleece.

Jason and Medea had to disembark from the *Argo* to purify themselves for the murder of Apsyrtus, since otherwise the talking head refused to sail on. They went to *Aeaea*, the island where *Circe*, Medea's aunt and great sorceress, lived. She purified them with the blood of a young swine, and they left to find the others. This delay meant that the Colchians' boat, commanded by Aeetes, managed to intercept them on the small isle of *Macris*, in Corcyra, where the Argonauts had been received by King *Alcinous* and his wife *Arete*. The Colchians claimed back Medea and the Golden Fleece, but the Argonauts refused. To avoid bloodshed in his peaceful kingdom, the King promised to come up with a solution the following day. Neither the

Meleager.

Queen nor the King managed to sleep, wondering what solution there could be to the delicate business. Finally, they arrived at a conclusion: "If Medea is still a virgin, she will return to Colchis; if she no longer is, she will remain together with Jason."

When the relieved King fell into a deep sleep, the Queen rushed to warn Jason and Medea of the result of Alcinous' decision. They held the wedding immediately in the cave of Macris, performed by Aristaeus' daughter, who was also Dionysus' nanny. Following the banquet, the newly-weds consummated the marriage on the Golden Fleece. The following morning, as a consequence, the troubled Colchians were unable to carry out Aeetes' orders and neither could they return to their homeland, since their King had forbidden their return unless they brought back his daughter. As a result, some of them established themselves in Corcyra, and others took occupation of the Ilirian islands.

Rounding Cape Malea, they passed in front of the islands of the *Sirens,* whose seductive singing attracted mariners to the reefs. However, thanks to the melodious music of Orpheus' lyre, much superior to that of the Sirens, they counteracted their evil power, and the *Argo* continued unharmed on its way. Butes alone jumped into the water to swim to the coast. But Aphrodite, having fallen in love with him, picked him up, taking him to Sicily, where she made him her lover.

Once safe, when they thought nothing else could happen to them, there was a huge storm and a great wave that threw land inside. The *Argo* was suddenly lifted into the middle of the Libyan Desert, and the Argonauts thought that was the end. Nevertheless, the Triple Goddess of Libya appeared to Jason in his dreams and showed him how to escape. Using the fifty oars as rollers, they put the *Argo* on top of them and pushed her. This arduous task took twelve days, and they would have died of thirst if they hadn't have found a spring Heracles had burst years before when he was going to the garden of the Hesperides. On the journey, Mopsus died from a Libyan snake's bite and Canthus at the hands of a shepherd protecting his sheep.

126

When they finally arrived at the Mediterranean coast, they launched the battered *Argo* and headed for the island of Crete, where they came across *Talos*, the bronze guard giant created by Hephaestus, who threw rocks at them, as was his custom to prevent boats passing there. Medea coaxed him with sweet words and false promises of immortality if he drank a magic potion, which in fact, was a soporific drink. The gullible metal giant drank it and immediately fell into a deep sleep. Medea took advantage of the situation and took out a bronze screw that sealed the only vein in his body, from where the colourless liquid that acted as his blood flowed out, and he died.

Apsyrtus' death

After a stop in Aegina, they arrived exhausted and worn out at Iolcus. Surprised that no one was there waiting for them, an old seaman told them everything that had transpired in the city during their absence. Pelias, certain the expedition had failed and all were dead, since those were the rumours from Thessaly, had executed Jason's parents, Aeson and Alcymedes, and his younger brother, *Promachus*, born after the *Argo* had left.

Jason became extremely angry after hearing the story, and he summoned a war council, where he asked for help to kill the treacherous Pelias. However, they all excused themselves, saying that they were very few and weak after the journey. Only *Acastus*, Pelias' son, had a good reason not to support Jason. Medea calmed her husband down and assured him that she herself would topple the evil king.

She spread the rumour that the great sorceress Medea had arrived at Iolcus and that she was capable of rejuvenating old people. Pelias' daughters, *Alcestis, Evadne,* and *Amphinome,* whose father was very aged by then, searched for her and asked her to rejuvenate their aged father. So Medea told them that first they should quarter him and then boil him in a gold cauldron with specific herbs. Then, with her magic, she would bring him back to life completely rejuvenated. Only Alcestis refused to spill her father's blood, even though it was to rejuvenate him. But Evadne and Amphinome, completely persuaded by Medea, took advantage of their father's sleeping to quarter him. Once his limbs had boiled in the cauldron, Medea refused to intervene.

The whole country turned against Jason and his wife, as a result of which he had to accept his cousin *Acastus*' claim to the throne while he was exiled. Evadne and Amphinome were also expelled from the kingdom, and they went to *Mantinea*, where they were purified. As for Alcestis, she married *Admetus* of Pherae.

Jason and Medea first visited *Orchomenos*, in Boeotia, where they hung the Golden Fleece in the temple of Zeus. They finally left the *Argo* beached on the Isthmus of Corinth, where it was dedicated to Poseidon. After that, they moved to Corinth, where they lived happily for ten years, until the day Jason fell in love with *Glauce*, King Creon's daughter. He then abandoned Medea, who had borne him two sons, *Pheres* and *Mermerus*, and then organised his wedding with the young princess.

Rejected and humiliated, Medea told Jason that breaking the promise he made in Aea, in the name of all the gods, was going to cost him dearly. But Jason ignored her threat and continued with his plans. So Medea made everyone believe she had accepted the situation, and as a peace offering, she sent to the bride a crown and a white tunic she had embroidered herself. As soon as the trusting girl put them on, inextinguishable flames lit upwards and not only burnt Glauce, but destroyed the entire palace, where all perished, burnt alive, except for Jason, who was able to escape the flames by leaping from a window over a pool.

Dissatisfied with her terrible revenge, Medea sacrificed her two sons to then flee on a chariot pulled by winged serpents. Some mythologists tell how Medea sacrificed her two sons according to Hera's instructions, who had promised her that, in this way, her sons would enjoy eternal life. Before she left, she prophesied that the *Argo* would cause Jason's death.

Medea went to Athens, as she was denied hospitality in Thebes. In Athens, she married King *Aegeus*, with whom

Medea.

she had a son. She was later exiled by *Theseus*, who found her guilty of trying to poison him. Then she returned to Colchis, since she found out her father had lost the throne when he had chased after her. His brother, *Perses*, had taken advantage of his absence to seize the kingdom. Medea reconciled with her father, and after her uncle's death, she returned to reinstate Aeetes on his throne.

While this was happening, Jason wandered from one place to another, scorned by all, since he had lost the favour of the gods. He used to sit beside the *Argo* remembering his singular voyage with the Argonauts. But one day, just as Medea had predicted, after a gust of wind, the stern fell on to his head, immediately killing him. Poseidon placed the stern of the *Argo* among the stars. Medea, however, didn't die, but returned immortal and ruled the *Elysian Fields* together with *Achilles*.

Analysis of the myth

According to some mythologists, the expedition of the Argonauts is a symbol for the first long-distance sea voyages that the Greeks went on for commercial reasons. The Golden Fleece could represent the countless riches they found in the East. Others believe this incredible journey is the image of the colonisation of the Black Sea and Asia Minor or even the symbol of the discovery of Caucas' (the ancient city of Colchis) marvellous gold mines, represented by the Golden Fleece.

According to mythological tradition, Jason's failure lies in the fact that he was assisted by Medea, representing the dark world of magic, powers that are totally against the rational spirit of the Greeks. Both Jason and Medea have inspired many works of art and literature. In 1661, Pierre Corneille wrote the political work titled "La Toison d'or" ("The Golden Fleece"), coinciding with Louis XIV's marriage to Marie Therese of Austria. Curiously, the Order of the *Golden Fleece* had been annexed before by the Austrian and Spanish Hapsburgs, the explorers of the New World, where they had gone in search of prized gold.

The Order of the Golden Fleece, founded in the fifteenth century by Phillip III, the Good, was inspired by the Golden Fleece myth. In the Middle Ages, the myth of Jason was taken up once more in the theme of the fraternity struck up between the Argonauts and in the adventures and dramas they lived to obtain the power of gold. Alchemists thought they would see on the Golden Fleece the parchment where the necessary cabalistic formulas had been written to turn lead into gold. Then chivalric orders were created, such as that of King Arthur and the Knights of the Round Table, whose mission was to recover the Holy Grail; or that of the Golden Fleece, which was under the protection of Saint Andrew.

Inspired by the myth of Jason, Cyrano de Bergerac imagined Jason going to the bowels of Hell, where he met some Spanish aristocrats, also searching for the prized Golden Fleece. By the twentieth century, Elémir Bourges wrote "La Nef" ("The Nave"), in which Bourges associates Prometheus with the expedition of the Argonauts and the power of fire with that of gold, both paths examples of the all-powerful.

More than two hundred literary adaptations have been written about Medea. Euripides took charge of the original work, and it features as one of his most pathos-filled tragedies. We should also mention Seneca, who emphasised the most supernatural aspects of the myth. Later, we can quote, among others, Corneille (1635) and Jean Anouilh (1946).

These charges at first did Theseus preserve with constant mind;
but then they left him, as clouds driven by the breath of the winds
leave the lofty head of the snowy mountain.
But the father, as he gazed out from his tower-top,
wasting his longing eyes in constant tear-floods,
when first he saw the canvas of the bellying sail.

Catullus

4. THESEUS

Pandion, King of Athens, was expelled from his kingdom and sought refuge in *Megara,* where he married *Pylia,* King *Pylas'* daughter, whom he succeeded to the throne. From this union, four sons were born: *Aegeus, Pallas, Nisus,* and *Lycus.* Years later, the eldest, Aegeus, aided by his three brothers returned to Athens and regained the throne. The new king had two wives: *Meta, Hoples'* daughter, and *Chalciope, Rhexenor's* daughter. However, while his brother, Pallas, had over fifty children, the *Pallantids,* he had no heir.

At one point, he visited Troezen, where he met a beautiful, young princess. The graceful maiden was *Aethra,* King *Pittheus'* daughter, who had been promised to *Bellerophon* before he fell into disgrace. Destiny had it that they would both fall in love and share a bed for three days, at the end of which they said goodbye, never to see each other again, since Aegeus was a married man. However, Aegeus had a premonition, and before leaving, he left his sword and sandals beneath a great rock crevice and asked Aethra, if a boy was born from their union, to raise him without revealing his origin until the day he was capable of lifting that rock. Then the young man should go to Athens to be reunited with him, where he would be recognised as his son.

After nine months, Aethra gave birth to a boy in a place called Genetlium, between the city and the port of Troezen. The boy, named Theseus, was raised by Aethra and his grandfather, Pittheus, in Troezen, and a certain *Cannidas* was his tutor. From a young age, Theseus demonstrated he was a strong, brave, and wise young man, as a result of which, people speculated on the possibility that his father was a god, and some people assert that he was engendered by *Poseidon,* the he most adored and honoured, from whom he received divine protection. To display his valour, a legend tells how the hero Heracles arrived at Pittheus' court to have a rest. During the banquet, he took off his lion-skin and threw it carelessly over a bench at the very same moment as the palace children came in. They though it was a lion and ran away in terror. Only seven-year old Theseus stayed; he took out his sword and set to attack the skin.

When he turned sixteen, his mother thought the time had come to reveal to him his origin. She did so and led him to the rock, known as the Altar of Zeus the Strong, which was on the road between Troezen and Hermione. It was not difficult to move the rock, under which he found Aegeus' sandals and sword. Ignoring his mother and grandfather's advice, Theseus was determined to walk to Athens, a journey that, contrary to the trip by sea, entailed all kinds of perils. So it was that Theseus, emulating his cousin Heracles, whom he admired, demonstrated to his father and his people his valour and bravery.

The deeds of Theseus

Upon arriving at *Epidaurus,* Theseus was forced to fight the lame giant *Periphetes,* son of *Hephaestus* and *Anticlea.* The giant, crippled monster used a bronze crutch to walk. He also used that crutch to strike travellers, knocking them out. Despite Periphetes' huge body, Theseus took little time to defeat him, and snatching his crutch, he struck him until he died. From then on, Theseus carried the crutch with him everywhere as a mace, which, in his hands, gained the power to kill whoever it struck.

When they arrived at the Isthmus of Corinth, he met *Sinis, Polypemon's* son, who was nicknamed *Pitiocamptes,* or bender of pine trees. This bandit was so strong, he could bend the tops of pine trees until they touched the ground. He had the custom of asking some traveller to help him in his task. When the innocent victim was holding the top of the pine tree, Sinis let go, and the unfortunate victim was shot into the air, crashing against the rocky side of the mountain. Another of his pastimes was to bend over two facing pine trees, in such a way that he could tie the victim to each of the trees. The trees, when they separated from each other so suddenly, tore the individual into two.

Theseus, already forewarned, skilfully avoided his strategy, and for the first and the last time, Sinis was the one who ended up being tied to each tree and, subsequently, torn apart. Just at that moment, Theseus saw a beautiful girl running to a field of asparagus. It was *Perigune,* Sinis' daughter, fleeing, because she believed she would share the same fate. Theseus calmed her down, since he intended her no harm. Both youngsters looked at each other and fell in love; they lay in the field of asparagus and engendered *Melanippus.*

A little later, he arrived at an extremely narrow part of the Isthmus of Corinth, where the only practical road was blocked by *Sciron, Pelops'* son. This brigand enjoyed himself by making passers-by wash his feet; when they bent over to do so, he threw them into the sea, where a giant turtle was waiting to devour them. Theseus refused to wash his feet, picked him up from the rock he used to sit on, and threw him into the sea, where he was devoured by the turtle he used to feed.

After that, in Crommyon, he hunted and killed an enormous, wild sow that was wreaking havoc in the region, terrorising everyone to such an extent, the inhabitants had stopped working the soil for fear of being attacked. Before arriving in Athens, he had to face *Cercyon,* the Arcadian, also known as 'the fighter', since he challenged all those he met in his path to fight with him; he crushed them to death with his powerful arms. Theseus caught him by surprise, and lifting him by the legs, he threw him to the ground, breaking his skull. It is said that Theseus was the creator of the free fight, in which skill counts for more than strength.

Finally, Theseus had to confront *Procrustes,* Sinis' father, when arriving in Attica. The giant, living by the side of the road on the way to Athens, entertained himself by inviting passers-by into his house, where he had two beds: one large and one small. If the traveller was short, he placed him on the big bed, where he stretched their limbs on a rack until they reached the right size. On the other hand, if the traveller was tall, he accommodated them on the small bed and cut their limbs to the size of the bed. Just as he did with the other ruffians, Theseus gave him a taste of his own medicine: the treatment he offered the poor travellers. First he lay him on the big bed and cut off his limbs, then he lay him on the small one and stretched his already amputated members, and finally he killed him.

When he finally arrived in Athens, his fame preceded him, and everybody was talking about him and his deeds. Before entering the city, he was purified in the Cephissus River and also was informed that King Aegeus was to marry Medea, the sorceress abandoned by Jason. Displeased, he headed for his father's palace and asked to see the King.

Medea, who was informed first, since she was the one who truly held all the power, knew immediately that Theseus was Aegeus' son, and she feared for her position in the palace. To get rid of him, she explained to Aegeus that an assassin had arrived with schemes to usurp the throne under false motives. She convinced him to receive him with gala in order to later poison him during the banquet. So it was done, and Theseus, clearly demonstrating his proverbial caution, accepted the false hospitality and said nothing of the reasons that had brought him to Athens.

During the banquet, Medea offered Theseus a glass of wine into which she had poured a poison brought from Acherusia, in Bithynia. It is told how servants then brought the roast, and Theseus unsheathed his sword to carve it. The King's eyes locked on the sword, and he recognised it as the same he had left under the rock. He got up suddenly and embraced Theseus, publicly declaring that that young man was his son. Immediately thereafter, he accused Medea of having tried to murder his own son and cast her aside. The sorceress mounted her chariot, pulled by dragons, and set off for the Black Sea.

Then sumptuous banquets were held in honour of Theseus. The fires on all the altars were lit, as well, and the glorious deeds of the new prince were sung. But not all were joyous at the good news. The Pallantids saw how the throne of Athens was slipping through their fingers, and they conspired to end their cousin's life.

Their strategy was as follows: twenty-five of the Pallantids and a large number of their partisans, led by Pallas himself, advanced on the city from Sphettus; the

135

other twenty-five waited in ambush in Gargettus. However, Theseus was informed about the plans by *Leos*, a herald who supported him, and surprising the ambush party, he annihilated them with his great mace, and Pallas found himself forced to plead for peace. However, Theseus had to leave the city for a year to purify himself.

But there is another deed to tell of Theseus, although researchers can never agree on when it actually happened. Some say that it was Medea who, to get rid of Theseus, gave him the task of killing the white bull of Marathon; others claim that Theseus liberated the Athenians from this wild bull to make amends with his people for the murder of the Pallantids. The enormous beast had been brought by Heracles from Crete in his seventh labour and set free on the plain of Argos. On its path to Marathon, it had killed hundreds of men. Theseus, trumpeting his skills, grabbed the bull by the horns and pushed it to the temple of Apollo, where he sacrificed it to the god.

Years later, *Androgeus,* King Minos of Crete and Pasiphae's son, arrived in Athens to participate in the Pan-Athenian games. The young prince proved to be a magnificent athlete, and he was victorious in all the events. That victory belied Athenian pride, and the competitors, supported by King Aegeus, killed the Cretan prince. For revenge, Minos razed and besieged the Athenian coast. However, this did not seem sufficient punishment, and he pleaded Zeus to pronounce an exemplary punishment. The god, sharing Minos' grief, since he was the son he had with Europa, sent plagues and earthquakes against Attica.

The kings of the region united and consulted the oracle of Delphi, receiving the order to compensate Minos as he requested. From then on, Athenians were forced to send seven young men and seven maidens to Crete as a tribute every nine years to be eaten by *Minotaur.*

As it happened, that same year, a new tribute was due to be sent to Crete for the third time, and Athenians cried and complained of their misfortune and asked Theseus to help them. He felt great pity for them, both for the parents and the children, and he offered to go to Crete in place of one of the young men. Aegeus refused, since he was not prepared to lose his only son, now that they finally had been united. But Theseus explained that he felt obliged to help what was now his people, and moreover, he believed he could defeat the Minotaur so this cruel demand would end.

Since the ship sailed under black sails, Aegeus proposed to his son, should he be victorious, to hoist, as a sign of victory, a white sail that he gave him. With this said, Theseus left with the other youths to the Island of Crete.

The Minotaur

On its voyage to the island, the deathly ship came across the bronze giant *Talos*, who, according to some, was the work of Hephaestus. He circled the island three times every day, jealously guarding against anybody landing there. He stoned them or burnt them on contact with his explosive body, after having spent hours under the burning sun. When Talos saw the black sails he recognised it as the tribute boat and let it pass. However, other researchers don't recognise this fact, justifiably, since the giant supposedly was killed at the hands of Medea when she returned with Jason to Iolcus. But it also can be supposed that, considering he was a robot, he was 'repaired' and restored by his creator.

When they arrived on the Cretan coast, Minos himself went down to the beach to personally inspect the new goods, to ensure that he was not being deceived by the Athenians. According to the legend, Minos took fancy of a beautiful Athenian maiden and would have enjoyed her if Theseus hadn't intervened. He challenged the monarch, assuring him that, as Poseidon's son, he could not allow such an act. So Minos, throwing his ring into the sea, challenged him to prove it true by retrieving his ring. There are differing opinions about this fact as well: some say that the *Nereids* and others that *Amphitrite* herself helped him find the ring, but the fact of the matter is that, when Theseus emerged from the water, he had the ring in one hand and Amphitrite's crown in the other.

Perhaps that was when *Ariadne,* having come down to the beach with her father, fell in love with Theseus. That

137

same night, cloaked in darkness, Ariadne entered the prison where Theseus was sleeping. There she made him promise that he would take her to Athens and marry her in exchange for her help. Theseus was grateful for her help and promised to do as she wished. She then gave him a ball of wool and told him he should tie the end to the gate and keep the other end in his hand throughout the labyrinth. Once he had killed the Minotaur, the thread of wool would show him the way out, while he rolled up the ball again.

The following morning, the fourteen youths were taken in front of the labyrinth where the Minotaur was enclosed. Minos, who was still offended by the way Theseus had stood up to and defeated him, asked him to demonstrate his courage by going first. The hero willingly accepted, since that was exactly what he had intended, and he went in to the labyrinth. Just as Ariadne had explained to him, the young man tied the end of the ball and started walking. The ball of wool enabled him to know whether he had or hadn't been that way already, and after a couple of hours, he started to notice scattered human bones that told him he was near the beast. A few metres further, he found the monster, the most revolting, horrific creature he had ever seen. Once again, the versions differ at this point: one tells how Theseus found the Minotaur asleep and killed him with blows; another tells that Theseus fought with the monster, against whose strength he had resort to all his wile and abilities, and after a long and hard struggle, he killed him with a sword Ariadne had given him the night before, along with the ball of wool he had skilfully hidden it in his clothes.

After killing the beast, Theseus went back on his steps with the help of the ball of wool and, before the stupefied gaze of the king, emerged victorious from the labyrinth. Ariadne could not contain her delight and ran into his arms. After a courageous battle, Theseus and the other youths, helped by Ariadne, managed to get out to sea, and they escaped. On their way, they met Talos once more, who prohibited them from passing. But Theseus, with a single, precise blow of his magic mace, made him lose his balance. Hours later, they stopped at an island called *Dia* and, later still, at one called *Naxos*. The youths disembarked to rest and admire the beauty of the island, and Ariadne parted from the group and fell asleep. Once again, there are differing versions: one tells how Theseus had fallen for some Athenian girl or that he reflected on the inconvenience and scandal the arrival of the Cretan princess would cause; another version tells that it was Dionysus who, in his dreams, asked him to leave her there, because he was in love with her. Whatever the case may be, since, truth be told, it will always be a mystery, the fact is that Theseus left without Ariadne, and when she awoke to discover that Theseus, breaking his word, had abandoned her, she burst into grievous tears. That was when Dionysus appeared before her, declared his love, and after little time, they married on that spot. Ariadne wore Amphitrite's crown, given to her by Theseus, as nuptial jewellery, and on her death, Dionysus placed it in her honour among the stars.

It is told how, although happy to have married Dionysus, Ariadne asked Zeus to avenge her, and he made Theseus, euphoric with victory, forget to raise the white sail. When Aegeus made out the boat with black sails, he believed his son had died, and devastated with grief, he threw himself into the sea and died. From then on, this sea has been called the Aegean in his honour.

Theseus' reign

Theseus' happiness was marred by the sad news, a fact that marked the rest of his life. Overwhelmed with pain and remorse, Theseus was proclaimed King of Athens, promising that, in memory of his father, he would try to be a good monarch. To ensure peace in his kingdom, he had all his opponents killed. He reinforced his rule as the fairest, wisest king of Athens, promoting the policy of federalisation, which was the basis of well-being in the region of Attica. He was the first Athenian monarch to introduce currency, on which he stamped the image of a bull. He established the Isthmian Games, naming Poseidon their patron. He created social laws in favour of the poorest and acted as judge between the Ionians and their Peloponnessian neighbours, placing over the disputed border the famous column which reads on the east side: "This is not Peloponnesus but Ionia!" and on the west side: "This is not Ionia but Peloponnesus!"

Several legends are told about Theseus during his reign. One of them tells how the Athenian hero participated, along with Heracles, in this triumphant expedition against the Amazons and obtained as spoils *Antiope*, an Amazon with whom he married, and they had a son, *Hippolytus*. Although there is another version, which seems more reliable if we compare it chronologically. According to this version, Theseus went to the land of the Amazons in a campaign against them and managed to kidnap their Queen, Antiope, with whom he fell in love. The Amazons, unaware that their Queen had married Theseus, lay siege to the city of Athens to reclaim her. There was a bloody war, in which many Amazons fell. The Athenians managed to repulse a foreign invasion for the first time. However, Antiope did not survive the battle. Some say she was killed by an arrow aimed at Theseus, others support the version that tells how Theseus himself killed her, since she was opposed to his marriage to *Phaedra*, Ariadne's sister.

Phaedra

As we can see, the myth of Theseus is full of mystery. Another enigma is when he married Phaedra. Some say that it was after Antiope's death, while others maintain that it was after his return from the Hells. Theseus certainly decided to marry Phaedra, Minos' youngest daughter, for two fundamental reasons: first, he wanted to secure a legitimate heir, since Hippolytus, considered a bastard son, was given to *Pittheus,* who adopted him as heir to the throne of Troezen; and second, to re-establish relations with Crete.

Phaedra had two sons with Theseus: *Acamus* and *Demophon*, but she never loved them. However, she fell in love with her stepson, Hippolytus, who, as the years went by, had become a handsome, virtuous young man. When he was visiting Athens to take part in the Isthmian Games and attend the Pan-Athenian Festivities, he was a guest at the palace and Phaedra used to watch how the young man trained naked. She gazed at him from atop the temple built in honour of watchful Aphrodite. She kept this incestuous love secret until she could not bear it a second longer, and she sent him a message in which, in addition to declaring her passion for him, she insulted Theseus, accusing him of using and killing women, giving the example of his treatment of her sister Ariadne or his own mother Antiope, and she incited him to betray Theseus and run away with her.

Hippolytus, horrified by the contents of the letter and out of love for his father, first burnt the letter and then entered Phaedra's room, shouting all kinds of reproaches at her. In despair and seeing no other way out, she tore off her clothes and screamed at the same time, accusing him of having tried to rape her. Theseus didn't bother to ask his son if that accusation was true and believing him, guilty cursed him and asked Poseidon to punish him. Taking advantage of the fact that Hippolytus was fleeing back to Troezen along the coast, Poseidon sent a huge tidal wave. A sea monster emerged, terrorising the steeds, which bolted, crashing the cart and throwing the innocent Hippolytus onto a reef and killing him.

Ovid and Virgil tell how Artemis, highly indignant at the death of Hippolytus, her most fervent adorer – since he had inherited this devotion from his mother, asked her nephew *Asclepius*, son of Apollo and expert in medicine, to resuscitate him like he had done with *Chiron* and *Glaucus*. So Asclepius revived him, touching Hippolytus' chest three times with magical herbs while repeating certain psalms. Hippolytus came back to life and went to Italy, near Aricia to be precise, in a sacred wood, where he was associated with the god *Virbius*. And it is told that he refused to let the horses that killed Hippolytus into the wood. Hades, indignant at Asclepius taking away his subjects, demanded the doctor's death, and Zeus struck him with a lightning bolt.

When Phaedra learnt what had happened, she couldn't bear her remorse and grief at her love's death. She wrote a note telling Theseus the whole truth and hanged herself.

141

Upon reading his wife's confession, he understood his terrible error and the *filial* love his son professed for him. From the on, Theseus became a bitter, surly man and a harsh, tyrannical king, until he earned the scorn and hatred of the people that had once praised and loved him so well. He was exiled to the Island of Scyros, where he died forgotten. But once again, there are other interpretations that tell how he was disgraced later, when he returned from the Hells. He had gone there with pretentious determination to kidnap Persephone. But we need to know some other legends and legendary companions of this Athenian hero before we go into detail.

The adventures of Pirithous and Theseus

One of the most important people in Theseus' life was *Pirithous*, King of the Lapiths. For some, this monarch of Thessaly was the son of Zeus and for others, of *Dia* and *Ixion*. It is told that, jealous of the deeds Theseus had succeeded in, he challenged him to prove that he truly was invincible. As provocation, he stole Theseus' cattle, and Theseus declared war. However, when the armies of each king were face to face, preparing to attack, Pirithous felt seduced by the hero and lay down his arms, declaring himself his slave. Theseus must have felt something similar, because he approached him to embrace him. From then on, they were inseparable friends, and together they went on many adventures.

On one occasion, *Pirithous* married *Hippodameia,* daughter of *Adrastus,* King of Argos, and he invited his friend Theseus to the banquet. Heracles and the centaurs also attended. After drinking much wine, they got so drunk, they kidnapped the bride and tried to rape her. This incited a field battle, and the centaurs were forced to flee to near Mount Pindos. Heracles chased them there and continued to fight until he accidentally wounded Chiron, the wisest, fairest centaur, with an arrow soaked in the blood of the *Hydra of Lerna*. Rather than living a life tortured by terrible pains, he offered his immortality to Prometheus and died in peace.

Poor Hippodameia, however, did not enjoy a very long life, and Pirithous became, like Theseus, a young widower. Together, the friends decided to kidnap the beautiful *Helen* of Sparta, where she was still a girl, and they gave her to his mother Aethra, until she became a beautiful maiden, old enough to be married. In return for his help, Pirithous asked Theseus to go with him to Tartarus to kidnap the beautiful Persephone. The friends were planning on both marrying daughters of Zeus, since being immortal, they would be guaranteed a queen to share the throne with until the end of their days. Theseus agreed, and even at the risk of his own life, he went down to the Hells with his friend. During his absence, the *Dioscuri,* Helen's brothers, gathered together an army of Laconians and Arcadians and marched on Athens, where they laid siege until Helen was returned to them. They returned with her to Sparta and married her to *Menelaus*. They placed *Menestheus* on the throne of Athens.

Menestheus, son of *Peteus,* had been exiled years before, and when he rose to the throne of Athens, to build a bond with the people, like a great demagogue, he recorded all the nobles and the power they had lost because of the Federalisation of Athens. He made the poor see that they had been subjected to a foreigner with a mysterious past, who had brought them wars, left them impious, and besides, had abandoned them to follow a friend on wild adventures.

Rumours circulated that Theseus had died, and he, unaware of the progress of events, was together with Pirithous in the Hells and couldn't move. What happened was that Hades found out about the evil intentions of the two friends and decided to teach them a lesson. He received them with false hospitality and offered them a banquet. Without suspecting anything, both of them took a seat in some comfortable, luxurious chairs from which they could not get up. They were called the 'chairs of oblivion', since, when someone sat in them, they lost their memory.

143

Meanwhile, they were struck by the *Furies*, and so four long years went by until Heracles arrived, who, following *Euristheus'* orders, came to kidnap *Cerberus*. When he recognised them, he tried to set them free. Demonstrating his notorious strength, he managed to pull Theseus off his cursed seat, but a fair piece of his buttocks stayed stuck to the seat. They say this is why his descendents had fairly small bottoms. However, there was nothing Heracles could do to release Pirithous, since his guilt, being the one who had the foolish idea, was much greater, and he stayed there, never to return to Earth.

A little after his return from Tartarus, Theseus built an altar dedicated to Heracles the Saviour, as a sign of his gratitude. However, his happiness was short-lived, since, arriving back in Athens, he discovered Menestheus had conquered his throne and the love of his people, and the city was corrupted by division and sedition. Exhausted and weakened, both by age and the tortures he had suffered in Tartarus, Theseus decided to set sail for Crete, where he had been promised hospitality.

However, destiny had it that a storm would divert him to Scyros, an island near Euboea, where its king, *Lycomedes*, received him with great pomp. For some strange reason, one day they both went out to wander, and he tricked him into climbing to the top of a cliff and then pushed him over the edge. And so it was that Theseus died in the same way his father had. Lycomedes made everyone believe that Theseus had fallen accidentally while walking along the cliff, due to his state of drunkenness.

The Athenians repented their ingratitude towards Theseus too late. He was the greatest king they ever had and the greatest hero given to Athens. Guided by their belated remorse, they idolised him and constructed a magnificent temple in his honour on the Acropolis. His remains were returned to the city, where he has been considered ever since as a demigod. His temple is, today, a museum where different Greek relics can be admired.

In Greek mythology, there are still more legends about this great Athenian hero. They say he was involved in the main heroic deeds like, for example, the great Hunt of

144

Calydon, in revenge of the champions who fell in the battle of the Seven against Thebes, and according to what they say, the reason he didn't take part in the adventures of the Argonauts was because, at that time, he was trapped in Tartarus.

Analysis of the myth

As we have seen, the myth of Theseus is full of chronologically contradictory legends, and the versions of each one are varied. The great importance of this myth is clear though, and his presence passes into history; Athenians confirm his taking part in the battle of Marathon (490 BC).

Theseus and his family's mythical footprints are as dense and prolific as his legends. The myth of Ariadne, the prototype of the seduced and abandoned woman, was used, above all, from the sixteenth century, in operas such as "Lamento d'Arianna" by Claudio Monteverdi, which pays tribute to love's triumph. In the seventeenth century, it was Friedrich Handel who wrote "Arianna in Creta", in London; "Ariane", by Massenet, with libretto by Catulle Mendis, in France; "Ariadne auf Naxos", by Richard Strauss, with libretto by Hugo von Hofmannsthal, in Germany. And finally, in the twentieth century, Darius Milhaud composed "L'abandon d'Ariane", with a burlesque tone and revealing Dadaist and Surrealist influences.

Some writers see in Ariadne and Dionysus' wedding the resurrection and light in a happy madness, after the suffering caused by the abandonment and disillusion. The German philosopher Nietzsche interpreted the myth through Ariadne's seductive dance, in which he could see the labyrinth where Ariadne, representing humanity, gets lost and finds herself again.

The myth of the labyrinth has led to the curious expression 'Ariadne's thread', the thread the young woman uses to get out of a prison that has several roads, which arrive at cul-de-sacs; Ariadne's thread is the image of reason always triumphing.

The struggle between duty towards one's husband and passion for an incestuous love released the most inspiring Greek tragedy, together with Oedipus, Antigone, and Electra. The myth of Phaedra is intimately bound to that of her stepson, Hippolytus, considered as the model of filial duty. There's "Hippolytus", Euripides' tragedy, and Seneca's "Phaedra", since Sophocles' and another by Euripides have been lost. However, the myth was taken up again in the sixteenth and seventeenth centuries, in which the central character is Hippolytus. Authors such as Garnier, Pinelière, or Gilbert present Theseus' son as the prototype of honour, rigour, and chastity, confronted by the destructive passion of the incestuous Phaedra, who is the main character in Racine's work. This prolific French poet presents a Phaedra who is only guilty of the forbidden love she feels for her stepson. It is her servant *Oenone* who denounces Hippolytus, leaving Phaedra free of guilt.

Schools of psychology have considered the disruption caused in some women by menopause – these disruptions represent for the woman a kind of female castration, provoked by the loss of reproductive functions, but not erotic capacity. This process has been named the 'Phaedra complex'.

> *To that task your son will be entrusted,*
> *With his mighty heart to win his place in the heavens;*
> *Twelve labours must be performed, and terrible*
> *And brutal things to overcome, bestial men among the*
> *worst;*
> *And in Trachania, the funeral pyre*
> *Will purify his victims with fire;*
> *And he will ride between the stars and be*
> *Accepted as relative to those that envied him,*
> *And he will send those forms born in the dens*
> *To crush his destiny.*

> Theocritus

5. HERACLES

Hesiod tells of when the day came that Zeus wanted to father the greatest, mightiest of heroes to protect both men and the gods from misfortune. His mind bustling with prodigious plans, he left Olympus and searched for the woman worthy to be mother to the hero he wished to give to the world. He found none superior to *Alcmene*, to whom he gifted the glory of being mother to *Heracles*, or *Hercules* to the Romans.

Unlike Zeus' other affairs, Alcmene was selected to give birth to a hero and not for his pleasure. She was also the last mortal he slept with, and he honoured her so much that, rather than rape or force her, he disguised himself as Amphitrion, taking advantage of his absence, and courted he with gentle caresses and affectionate words of love.

On the following day, Alcmene slept with her real husband and conceived *Iphicles*. When she nearly had completed the nine months of pregnancy, Zeus boasted that, in a short time, he who was destined to be the most glorious hero of Greece, the mortal *Alcmene's* son, to be called Heracles, i.e., 'Hera's glory', was to be born. Upon hearing this, Hera asked Zeus to promise her that Perseus' descendent, to be born the following night, would be known as the supreme king of men. As soon as Zeus swore it by the Styx, Hera called her daughter *Ilythia*, and together they went down to earth.

First they went to Mycenae, where *Nicippe,* wife of King *Sthenelus*, Alcmene's uncle and Perseus' son, was in labour. Ilythia advanced her birth pains. Then they went to Thebes, where the goddess of maternity, crossing her legs in front of Alcmene's house delayed his birth until Hera informed her that *Eurystheus*, Nicippe's son, had been born. Heracles was born the following night, followed by his brother, Iphicles, an hour later.

Hera returned to Olympus boasting of her astuteness, and Zeus was furious when he heard the news. He was so angry, he had to punish someone and he expelled *Ate,* his eldest daughter. She must have been the one who told Hera what had happened. He seized her by her golden hair and threw her violently to Earth.

However, Hera was not content to see Heracles only relegated to second rung and she declared her unlimited hatred for him. They were just babies, Heracles and Iphicles, sleeping peacefully in their cradle, when the vengeful goddess sent them two enormous snakes. Iphicles' screams and crying awoke the parents, who discovered Heracles with a dead snake in each hand, displaying his divine nature. So it was that Hera discovered it would be useless to try to kill him, but she could bother him by putting all kinds of difficult, uncomfortable obstacles in his way.

Heracles' education was entrusted to the centaur Chiron, who taught him how to use different weapons and trained him in all types of sports; Amphitrion taught him the art of driving a chariot; *Eurythus* initiated him in the bow and arrow, and *Lynus* trained him in singing and playing the lyre. Heracles soon surpassed all his tutors and never met a rival to his skills. However, he was courteous by nature, and it is said that he was the first man to return the corpses of those he slew to their families to be buried.

At a very young age, he was looking after Amphitrion's flock of sheep when he performed the first of his famous deeds, killing the lion of Cytheron, which was wreaking havoc in his parents' and King Thespius' kingdoms. Astonished by the youth's feat, and as a reward for freeing them from the wild beast, Thespius offered him the favours of his fifty daughters. Some say that only one of them refused to sleep with him, and even so, Heracles fathered fifty one children, since the eldest and youngest daughters gave birth to twins.

From then on, Heracles wore the lion's skin and used the open jaws as a helmet. Then, he fought *Erginos*, a cruel king from Orchomenos who imposed a harsh tax on the kingdom of Thebes, and he killed him. *Creon*, King of Thebes, gave him his daughter *Megara's* hand in marriage as a reward. However, the hero's happiness infuriated Hera, and the marriage took a tragic turn. The goddess made the hero go insane so that, instead of seeing his family, he saw horrible

148

beasts. He strangled his wife and killed all the children he had with her, known as the *Alcides*. Some researchers claim that Heracles only killed his children.

When he came round and realised what he had done, he went mad again, this time with grief. After several months of solitude and pain, he was purified by King Thespius, and he went to Delphi to consult the oracle. The fortune teller advised him to go to Tiryns and serve Eurystheus for twelve years, performing every task that was asked of him. Although he didn't like in the least to be slave to anyone inferior to him, Heracles knew very well that he couldn't do anything against his destiny, and he presented himself at his cousin's court, who gave him the famous 'Twelve Labours'.

It has been told that the gods gifted him with different weapons and shields; however, he hated weapons and preferred to defend himself with a simple club or his bare hands. His nephew, *Iolaos*, served him as coachman, or squire, for the twelve years.

The first labour: the Nemean Lion

Eurystheus commanded him to kill that terrible beast, which could not be harmed by mortal weapons. Echidna and Typhon's offspring of was terrorising the inhabitants of the region of Peloponnesus. After confirming that neither arrows nor his sword could pierce the monster's hard skin, which was even capable of breaking his club in two, Heracles decided to fight the beast bare-handed. They say that when he approached the lion, it bit off one of his fingers, but the hero wasn't scared off, and trapping its head in his powerful arms, he crushed it until the lion was strangled to death.

He made a new club, and after a great deal of thought, it occurred to him to use the animal's claws to skin it and to make armour that no arrow could pierce. He made a new helmet from its powerful jaws.

The second labour: the Hydra of Lerna

This was another monster engendered by Echidna and Typhon, and it was raised especially by Hera to put an end to Heracles. The beast was found in the region of Lerna, near Argos. It had a prodigious body in the shape of a dog and nine snake heads, of which only one was immortal. They say it was so poisonous, its breath alone could kill.

Athena, always willing to help the hero, advised him to attack it while holding his breath. However, whenever he cut off one of the heads, two grew back in its place, and so it grew and grew. To make it even more difficult, Hera sent an enormous crab to snap his feet. The hero, furious at the interruption, crushed it with his club. Hera retrieved her loyal servant and placed it in the stars, creating Cancer's constellation.

Heracles finally resolved that he should find a way to stop more heads growing; he asked Iolaos to light him some torches, and when he cut a head off, he burnt the amputated end, preventing more from growing. Finally, he decapitated the hydra and buried the immortal head under a heavy boulder. Then he opened he beast's veins and dipped all his arrows in its poisonous blood. In that way, any wound, however slight, that he struck with his arrows would be fatal.

The third labour: the Ceryneian Hind

This animal, which some believed to be a stag and some a deer, was the fastest animal in all of Greece. Not even Artemis had succeeded in trapping it. Some state that its speed was such that it barely touched the ground. Its horns were made of gold and its hooves of bronze. Heracles was given orders to bring it back alive to Mycenae.

He had to chase it for one whole year. Finally, he managed to strike its front legs with one of his arrows in such a way that it passed clean through the bone and the tendon, and the wound did not bleed. He lifted it on his shoulder and arrived with it alive in Mycenae.

The fourth labour: the Wild Boar of Erymanthus

The fourth labour entrusted to the great hero was to capture alive a wild boar that lived in Erymanthus and wreaked havoc in the fields around Psophis. On his way to Erymanthus, Heracles found himself in the middle of a struggle among centaurs. He killed many of them with his poisoned arrows, but a slip-up caused him to wound his former tutor Chiron in the knee. No herbs or magic ointments helped him, and the wise centaur chose to die, giving his immortality to Prometheus. Later, the hero found the wild boar's tracks, and throwing a net over it, he managed to capture it. He tied it in chains and carried it onto his shoulders to Mycenae. They say that Eurystheus hid in a bronze vessel when he heard that Heracles was bringing the wild boar to show him.

The fifth labour: King Augeas' stables

Heracles was then ordered to clean out King Augeas of Elis' stables in just one day. These enormous stables hadn't been cleaned for years. The dirt gathered was tremendous, and the smell of manure infected all the air of Peloponnesus. Augeas was the richest man in all Greece, since he had the greatest number of cattle. Moreover, they were immune to illness, very fertile and never miscarried. The king promised a tenth of his cattle to Heracles if he succeeded in his task.

After studying the terrain and surroundings, Heracles saw that if he altered the course of the two rivers that went close-by the stables, the Alpheus and the Peneus, the strength of the current would clean the floor of the unworldly stables. He built a dyke to redirect the course of both, and the water went straight through the stables, washing away all the impurities and leaving them completely clean of dirt and smell. Once he had completed his task, he guided the rivers back to their natural courses.

However, the greedy king, certain of the hero's failure, refused him the agreed reward. Heracles, in a fit of anger, killed him and all his children, except *Phileus,* because he had been brave enough to defend him before his father.

The sixth labour: the destruction of the birds of Lake Stymphalus

These birds were a kind of giant eagle with beaks, claws, and wings of bronze. They were consecrated to Ares, fed on humans, and lived on the Lake Stymphalus in Arcadia. They killed men and animals thanks to their sharp feathers, and their excrement poisoned the earth where it fell.

To flush them from their swampy hiding place, Heracles followed Athena's advice once more, and using some cymbals, he struck up such a thunderous noise that the birds of prey were terrorised and took flight, forming an enormous flock. He quickly shot them with his arrows and managed to kill a great number of them. The rest fled in terror and took refuge on Ares' island in the Black Sea, where they were later discovered by the Argonauts.

The seventh labour: the Cretan Bull

This time, Eurystheus ordered Heracles to capture the white bull that Minos hadn't wanted to sacrifice to Poseidon and that had fathered the Minotaur with Pasiphae. As it happened, the god had rendered the bull insane, and the huge white beast was rampaging across the island of Crete, destroying harvests and threatening the inhabitants, causing famine.

After wrestling the beast with his bare hands, the hero managed to trap the bull by its horns, tame it, and then carry it to Greece. However, no one wanted to be responsible for looking after the bull, and it was set free. It was finally captured by Theseus at the gates of Marathon.

The eighth labour: the capture of Diomedes' mares in Thrace

Heracles had to seize the human flesh-eating mares of Diomedes, King of the Bistones, to fulfil this labour. The hero benefited this time from *Abdero's* help. Together they went to Thrace, where Heracles fought the bloodthirsty King and threw him, still alive, to the mares. These, hungry animals devoured him quickly. So, he mastered them without great difficulty. Heracles sadly realised, however, that his friend, Abdero, falling in the course of the combat, had also been eaten by the mares. After taming them, Heracles gave them to the wild animals that live in Olympus.

The ninth labour: the Queen of the Amazon's belt

Eurystheus had a daughter, *Admete*, who took delight in clothes and jewellery. When the spoilt princess learnt that *Hippolyte,* the Queen of the Amazons, had a beautiful gold belt, a gift from the god Ares as a symbol of power, she asked her father to order Heracles to bring it to her.

Heracles set off with Iolaos and, according to some versions of the legend, Theseus, among other volunteers. They disembarked at the port of Themiscyra, and he presented himself to Hippolyte, who invited her to stay because he felt attracted to her. She was attracted to him, and as proof of her love, she agreed to give him the magical belt.

However, Hera was not willing for Heracles to succeed so easily, and disguising herself as an Amazon, she spread the word that this foreigner's real intention was to assassinate the Queen. Thus, they attacked Heracles and his companions. The hero could do nothing but defend himself and even killed Hippolyte in the process; he took her belt, and they set off.

On their return to Eurystheus' court, they passed by Troy, where Heracles saw a young maiden, *Hesione*, was about to be eaten by a horrible sea monster. He killed the beast and rescued the young woman in exchange for a reward that *Laomedon*, her king and father, promised him. But he was not a man of his word, and once the monster was dead, he refused to give him the reward. Heracles took revenge by killing him and all his children, except Hesione, whom he offered his faithful companion Telamon, and her brother Priam, whom he placed on the throne.

The tenth labour: the capture of Geryon's oxen

Eurystheus ordered that his tenth task would be to capture and bring him the giant Geryon's oxen. This giant, son of Chrysaor and Callirrhoe, was king of the westernmost country of Greece, located beyond the known frontiers of the Earth (Spain). He had been born with three bodies joined at the waist and was famous for being the strongest man in the world. His immense, prized cattle was in the care of a shepherd called *Eurythion* and his dog *Orthus*, which had two heads and was son of Echidna and Typhon.

Upon arriving in Tartessos, Heracles raised two columns to leave his footprint on the journey, which he placed one facing the other: the first in Africa and the second in Europe. (These columns of Heracles tend to be identified with the Mount Abyla or Abylix, in Africa, and Mount Calpe, in Europe). There are other versions as well; for example they say that both continents were joined and that the hero opened a channel between the two, or on the contrary, some say that Heracles tried to shorten the distance between the two continents to stop whales and other sea monsters coming in.

It is also told that, irritated by the excessive heat, he threatened *Helios* with his arrows, and he, in order to pacify him, lent him a ship of gold, which enabled him to cross the ocean to Erythea. When he arrived at Mount Abas, *Orthus*, the dog, charged him down, but Heracles defeated it with a single blow of his club, leaving it lifeless. Eurythion attacked him immediately afterwards and met the same fate as his dog. While Heracles was taking the cattle, Geryon appeared and challenged him to a fight. The hero charged into Geryon's side and then, with just one arrow, shot through his three bodies. Thus he seized the oxen without demands or payment.

Then he returned through Gallia, Italy, and Thrace, having many adventures and finally arriving at Eurystheus' court, who sacrificed the oxen to Hera.

154

The eleventh labour: the golden apples of Hesperides

Up to that point, eight years and one month had gone by since Eurystheus had given him his first task. According to some researchers, the cruel king ordered him to do ten labours rather than twelve, but Eurystheus did not recognise as valid tasks either the second, since he thought that Heracles would not have killed the Hydra if it hadn't been for Iolaos' help, or the fifth, since Heracles had been contracted by Augeas, and as a result, he gave him two more.

The eleventh labour was to steal the golden apples that *Gaea,* Mother Earth, had gifted to Hera on the day of her wedding, under the protection of the *Hesperides, Atlas'* daughters, and the dragon *Ladon.* However, Heracles knew little more about the golden apples or where the garden they were guarded in was. After many journeys and interrogations, the hero discovered the path he should follow thanks to *Nereus*, Pontos and Gaea's son. This god advised him as well that he shouldn't gather the apples himself, rather he should arrange it so that Atlas was the one to do so.

When Heracles arrived where he could find the old Titan supporting the skies, he offered to free him of the weight for one whole day if he, in return, brought him the golden apples that his daughters guarded. The giant agreed, delighted at the idea of being free, if only for one day, but he asked him to first kill the dragon. He did so, with a single arrow, and when the Titan returned with the apples, he refused to take over his job again, declaring that he would take the apples to Eurystheus himself. But Heracles thought of a trick: he told the Titan that he agreed, but that he was very uncomfortable, and he would really appreciate it if, before he left, he could hold the skies for a few seconds so that he could put a pillow on his neck. The giant agreed, savouring his regained freedom, but then Heracles confessed to him he had fallen into his trap and went happily on his way with the apples.

On his way back, he bumped into the giant *Antheus*, Gaea and Poseidon's son, who challenged him to a duel. However, Antheus was not quickly defeated by Heracles, since every time he defeated him and threw him to the ground, the giant seemed to regain his strength and counterattacked with great impetus. Then, Heracles realised that the only way to beat him was by preventing the giant from touching the ground. So he lifted him into the air, broke his ribs, and held him until he died.

He also met *Prometheus,* whose intestines were being eaten by a *griffin* as an eternal punishment. Heracles remembered poor Chiron wanting to end his suffering from his incurable wound, and he offered them the following deal: given that Prometheus was destined to suffer until one of the immortals voluntarily went down to Tartarus, Chiron could voluntarily offer himself, ending his suffering and freeing Prometheus.

Finally, the apples were consecrated to Athena, who returned them to the Hesperides.

The twelfth labour: the kidnapping of Cerberus

As his last labour, it was also the most dangerous. Eurystheus ordered him to kidnap the three-headed dog, *Cerberus*, and bring him back from Tartarus to his palace. Eurystheus knew that no mortal had ever returned alive from Tartarus, and he was sure that he would never see his cousin again.

However, Heracles, assisted by Hermes and Athena, went down to the underworld, got Charon to take him across the Acheron River, and requested an audience with Hades. He listened with glee to the hero's words and gave him permission to take Cerberus if he succeeded in capturing him, since during those days, he had escaped his chains. Before setting off in search of the fearful dog, Heracles managed to free *Theseus* from the 'chair of oblivion', where he had spent several years unable to move. He succeeded in finding Cerberus, and after wrestling with him, he muzzled him and took him to Eurystheus, who, horrified, hid again in the bronze vessel and ordered him to take the monster straight back to the Hells.

* * *

Once he had completed the labours given by Eurystheus, Heracles regained his liberty. However, his happiness was cut short when he decided to look for a new wife. He then fell in love with *Iole,* daughter of King *Eurytus* of Oechalia and sister of Iphitus, one of the Argonauts who was thought to be the best archer among all there were. Eurytus promised his daughter's hand if the hero managed to beat Iphitus in an archery contest. Despite the precision of the Argonaut's arrow, Heracles won; but the King, fearing another attack of madness from the hero, refused to keep his word. Blind with rage, or through the workings of a new madness, Heracles killed Iphitus and had to flee.

To purify himself, he had to lose his freedom and serve as a slave in the court of Queen *Omphale* of Lydia, who enjoyed making the muscular hero dress up as a woman while she dressed in his lion-skin.

After being toy to Omphale's whims, Heracles remembered that, while in Tartarus, he had met the spirit of *Meleagros*, son of Aeneus, and he had advised him to marry his sister, *Deianeira*. However, she already had a suitor; the river god Achelous, a worthy opponent. The fight between the two forms an important myth. It is said that Achelous was able to take on any form he desired. After long hours of struggle, Achelous took on the form of a bull to charge Heracles. However, as he had done with the Cretan bull, the hero took him by the horns with such strength, he broke off one of the shafts. *Fortuna*, the goddess of plenty, took the horn and guarded it among all her treasures, with it taking on the name from then of the 'horn of plenty', and announced Heracles the winner.

The happy couple were overjoyed at the birth of their son Hyllus. However, at some point, Heracles got annoyed with a young relative of Aeneas called *Eunomus*, and not gauging his strength properly, he killed him accidentally. During his exile, while he was going to Trachia with Deianeira and Hyllus, they came to the river Evenus, whose level had risen very high. He was thinking about how to cross the river when *Nessus,* the centaur, turned up and offered to take Deianeira and Hyllus across while he swam. Heracles agreed with gratitude, and after throwing his bow and arrows to the other bank, he leapt in to swim across. Nessus took advantage, then, to run in the opposite direction and tried to rape Deianeira. His wife's screams alerted the hero, who, upon reaching the bank, picked up his bow and one arrow and killed the centaur.

Before he died, Nessus asked Deianeira to forgive him, and to demonstrate his good will, he offered her a recipe to create a love potion: "When you feel your husband's love for you weakening, mix the blood that flows from my wound with a little oil and spread it on his shirts." Deianeira thanked him for the advice and took a little of the blood that was flowing from the fatal wound of the centaur, putting it in a jar.

Once they were settled in Trachis, Heracles had new adventures. On one occasion, he remembered Iole and decided that the time had come to get his revenge with King Eurytus. He took the city of Oechalia and killed the King and his sons. Horrified at the death of her family, the beautiful Iole tried to kill herself, but she failed, and Heracles took her to Trachis. Once there, he asked his wife to prepare clean clothes for him to offer a sacrifice to Zeus. Deianeira, seeing her husband's passion for Iole, decided to use the love potion and filled her husband's shirt with it.

As soon as Heracles put the shirt on, he started to feel a suffocating heat, such that his skin started to burn. He tried to take off the top in vain, as it had become stuck to his body. He roared at his servants to make a funeral pyre on Mount Oeta, but they were paralysed as witnesses to the scene and could not react. It was Heracles himself that uprooted several trees to make a pyre upon which he then threw himself. Heracles entrusted his bow and arrows to *Philoctetes* and asked him to light the pyre. Once that was done, Heracles' soul lifted to the heavens and was collected by Zeus, who took it to Olympus. That was where Hera reconciled with him and offered him the hand of her daughter *Hebe*.

Hercules and the giant.

Hercules, the Roman hero

Heracles is much better known as *Hercules*, his Latin transcription. However, Latin writers enriched his many adventures with some extra episodes. So, for example, Hercules challenged the giant *Cacus,* who stole some oxen from the cattle he had robbed in turn from Geryon, or also King Faunus, a cruel sovereign who had the custom of killing any foreigner that ventured onto his land. Finally, he was received by *King Evander*, who founded a sanctuary in Rome in his honour.

For the Romans, Hercules was less fearsome than Heracles and was often accompanied by the muses and Apollo.

Analysis of the myth

Heracles/Hercules is the hero *par excellence*, as much in the Greek world as in the Latin one. A series of elements are combined in him that are common to all the great classical and modern-day heroes. It is the personification of the ideals of strength and conquest.

The myth of the hero is very important in society and for people. It establishes socially a collective identity, a motivating role. Individually, it contributes, above all, to the assertion of personality in childhood and adolescence.

Heracles/Hercules' character surpasses that of other heroes because it groups together several myths. All of them indicate an extraordinary strength and unbalanced feelings, greater than human capacity. Although he had many romantic affairs, his character is not that of the great lover, but the warrior. He is a solitary warrior, who rids the world of wild monsters and beasts from one border to another. He is the fighter of a period that only knows man-to-man fighting; he is not committed to a state, a people, or an idea. He is, in brief, the mythical representation of noble ideals. That is why the legends that narrate collective adventures in which Heracles participates are much later (Jason and the Argonauts, for example).

For the Greeks, Heracles was the symbol of strength and energy, and even unbeaten heroism. That is why the creation of the Olympic Games is attributed to him. He was adored, at the same time, as a man and a god. He represented, as well, the man of justice fighting against evil and harm, punishing impiety, and he became the model of valour faced with dangers of the unknown. The Greeks, finally, considered him the father of the inhabitants of Peloponnesus. In Rome, Hercules also took on the form of the agrarian and fertility god, since it was believed the hero favoured plentiful harvests, as he did the greatest vigour in human life.

His deeds inspired the enthusiasm of classic writers, such as Sophocles or Euripides in Greece and Seneca in Rome. This hero has become one of the subtlest characters passed on to us by mythology: sometimes so strong and brave, and, at other times, so fragile and human. He has inspired a large number of artists, become part of our language ("he's a Hercules" is said of an extremely strong person), and given his name to a constellation. Geographers call Gibraltar 'the columns of Hercules'.

"Whereon Hector spoke.
'Hear from my mouth," said he, "Trojans and Achaeans,
The saying of Paris, through whom this quarrel has
come about.
He bids the Trojans and Achaeans lay their armour
upon the ground,
While he and Menelaus fight in the midst of you for
Helen and all her wealth.
Let him who shall be victorious and prove to be the better man
Take the woman and all she has, to bear them to his own
home,
but let the rest swear to a solemn covenant of peace."

Homer

6. THE HEROES OF THE TROJAN WAR

I. Troy

Ilos, descendent of Dardanus and son of *Tros*, founded what was to be the capital of Troas; initially it was called Ilium and later, in memory of his father, *Troy*. Ilos was succeeded by his son *Laomedon*, who, with Poseidon and Apollo's help (having been punished by Zeus for rebelling against his wishes), constructed an immense wall around the city, which was protected by huge dykes. But once the work was finished, the King refused to pay the gods with the promised sacrifices. In revenge, Poseidon created a sea monster that flooded the fields with salt water and devoured the inhabitants, and Apollo sent an epidemic that killed many Trojans.

The people consulted the oracle, who declared the only way to pacify the fury of the gods was by sacrificing *Hesione*. So the Trojan monarch was forced to chain his daughter to a rock in the sea. However, fortune had it that at that moment *Heracles*, accompanied by *Telamon, arrived;* the hero offered to kill the monster, and in exchange, Laomedon offered him the two immortal white horses Zeus had gifted him as a reward for the abduction of Ganymedes. However, once more, Laomedon went back on his word and refused to deliver the agreed reward to the hero in return for the sea monster's death. Heracles also decided to take revenge; he hired an army and conquered the city. Then he killed the King and all his sons, except for *Priam*, who succeeded his father to the throne, and Hesione, who was given to Telamon as a bride.

Priam was known as at first as *Podarces*, which means 'light feet'. Heracles saved him from certain death, because he was the only one of Laomedon's sons that supported the hero against his father. They say his sister bought him, and from then on, he adopted the name Priam, which means 'he that was sold'. Once he had ascended to the throne, he took Arisbe as his wife and then *Hecuba*.

When he was still young, he supported the Phrygians in combat against the Amazons. However, when the Trojan War broke out, he was already an old man. According to Homer, Priam had a great number of children, *Hector, Paris, Deiphobus, Cassandra, Creusa, Laodice* and *Helen*, many of whom played important roles, and some say decisive, in the Trojan War.

II. Paris

Hecuba was pregnant with Paris when she had a strange dream in which she gave birth to a torch or lit flame that came out of her stomach and burnt her and all of Troy. The following morning, she told her dream to her husband, and he, believing it to be a premonition, went to consult the oracle. The oracle declared that Paris would cause the fall of Troy, which would be besieged, destroyed, and burnt to the ground. Hearing the oracle thus speak, the royal couple decided, for the good of Troy, to abandon the new-born in a wood near Mount Ida. However, the boy didn't die, rather he was taken in by a shepherd called Agelaus.

Paris grew strong and healthy and became a handsome young man. He fell in love with *Oenone*, a lovely nymph, who loved him in return. This nymph, daughter of the river god Cebren, received a gift from the god Apollo: that of preparing potions with medicinal plants. However, this adolescent love didn't last long.

One day when Paris was watching the flock, *Hera, Athena,* and *Aphrodite* told him he had been declared judge for the following trial: he had to choose who should receive the golden apple with the inscription 'To the most beautiful', which *Eris*, the goddess of Discord, had thrown during *Thetis* and *Peleus'* wedding. In order to convince the stunned young man to choose her, Hera promised him power, Athena, wisdom, and Aphrodite the love of the most beautiful woman in Greece. So without hesitation, Paris offered the apple of discord to the goddess of Love.

To keep her promise, Aphrodite sent the young man to Troy, where he met his real parents, who accepted him gracefully, and from whom he obtained a fleet which he sailed to Greece. Meanwhile, Hera and Athena swore vengeance.

Although, Paris felt no scruples at leaving Oenone, who could read the future in people's eyes. In Paris' eyes, she saw his tragic end and tried to dissuade him from marrying her rival. Seeing that he refused to listen to her, she told him that, come what may, he could always count on her, since she could cure him should he be injured.

Young Paris arrived in Troy, where he took part in some Funeral Games and where his athletic talent shone, attracting the attention of *Cassandra*. This beautiful princess, daughter of Priam and Hecuba, had been courted by Apollo, who, hoping his love to be requited, had given her the gift of prophecy. However, she did not agree to his desires, and unable to withdraw the gift, he made it so that no one would ever believe her infallible prophecies.

Cassandra told her parents that there was a young man who resembled the family extraordinarily, and then she went into a prophetic trance and predicted that he would bring ruin to Troy. The royal couple, happy to see that their son had not died, scoffed at the prophecy and received him with open arms, promising to make up his sad, impoverished past by conceding to all his desires. Paris didn't hesitate and asked for a fleet to sail to Greece.

III. Helen

Leda, King *Tyndarus* of Sparta's wife, was seduced by Zeus, disguised as a swan. From this double union, Leda had four children: *Helen* and *Polydeuces*, Zeus' children and immortal as a consequence, and *Clytemnestra* and *Castor*, sons of Tyndarus. Helen was gifted with all the blessings of beauty, and her fame spread across all of Greece. However, her destiny was so harmful for the Greeks that some assert her mother was *Nemesis*, the goddess of revenge.

When she was still a girl, she was kidnapped by *Theseus*. Taking advantage of his absence, who had descended to the

Hells, her brothers, Castor and Polydeuces, the Dioscuri, rescued her and then abducted *Aethra*, Theseus' mother, to work as a slave in Helen's service.

In Sparta once more, Helen received one hundred proposals of marriage. One of her suitors, Odysseus or *Ulysses*, to attract the King's favour, skilfully convinced him to make all the suitors take a solemn oath: that they would promise to accept Helen's choice and swear to protect both Helen and her future husband, should it prove necessary. In that way, Tyndarus would be certain that no matter what his stepdaughter's choice, no one would try to kidnap her or murder her husband.

Helen chose from among all the suitors, the most noble, attractive, powerful, and courageous in all Greece, *Menelaus*, who was to become successor to the Spartan throne. Their marriage was happy for many years, and their happiness was at its height with the birth of a daughter, *Hermione*. Then the Trojan Prince Paris arrived, hospitably received by the royal couple. Helen's mature beauty conquered Paris' heart, and Aphrodite kept her promise, making her fall in love with him. Taking advantage of Menelaus' absence, Paris abducted Helen and took her to Troy. When her husband returned and found out what had happened, he quickly sent messengers in all directions to call together the former suitors and to call on their oaths. They all came except for one, Ulysses.

IV. Ulysses

Descendent of *Autolycus*, son of Hermes, Ulysses is Greece's most famous hero, alongside Heracles. He was born on the island of Ithaca, and his parents were *Laertes*, King of the island, and *Anticlea*. His grandfather Autolycus taught him to fight with his fists to defeat his adversaries. It is also told how he robbed a magical helmet to give to his grandson, which allowed the hero to enter Troy without being seen.

Ulysses undertook many journeys during his adolescence, above all to visit his grandfather Autolycus. During one of these visits, they went hunting together on Mount Parnasse. Ulysses was wounded by a wild boar in one knee; the resulting scar enabled his wife, years later, to recognise him. After that, he visited King Iphitus, one of the Argonauts and companion of his grandfather, who also took part in the expedition, and was a famous, fearsome archer. This king gifted Ulysses with Eurytus' trusty bow, which fired unstoppable arrows.

When he reached adulthood, Ulysses decided to marry. First he chose Helen, but after he was rejected, he married the peaceful *Penelope*, daughter of the King of Icaria, with whom he had his beloved son, *Telemachus*. A little after his son's birth, Menelaus' messenger *Palamedes* came, asking him to join the expedition and thus comply with his oath. But Ulysses didn't want to leave his pleasant, peaceful life together with his beloved wife and son, so he decided to pretend insanity and started to plough the sea and sow salt. Palamedes, son of *Nauplius*, in order to confound his plan, put Telemachus in front of the yoke, and in order not to kill him, Ulysses had to turn the oxen. This proved that Ulysses was only pretending, and he had to join the Greeks, but not without first swearing vengeance.

The hero was sent to Troy as ambassador to reclaim Helen peacefully. However, he was unsuccessful, and the Greeks decided lay siege on Troy. They consulted the oracle and were told that the task would only prove successful with Achilles' help.

V. Achilles

Thetis, daughter of Nereus and Doris, was, without a doubt, the most famous and beloved Nereid. She was famous for her sweetness and sense of hospitality. Zeus and Poseidon courted her, but then, *Themis*, goddess of Prudence, prophesied that Thetis' son would be more powerful than his father, and before running the risk of being forced to give their power to the son that they would have with her, they decided to give her to *Peleus*, King of Aegina, as wife. This mortal king had been secretly in love with the nereid, and the idea made him very happy. However, Thetis did not feel the same, and although at first she resisted him, she ended up complying with her destiny.

The wedding was celebrated with great pomp; all the gods attended the banquet except for Eris, the goddess of Discord, who threw a golden apple there and cause the war between the three goddesses, and subsequently, the Trojan War.

Thetis only had one son with Peleus, *Achilles*, who was raised with much love. In order for her son to be invulnerable, she took him to the banks of the River Styx, whose waters had the power to make everything that touched them invincible to any wound. She held the boy by his heel and ducked him in the river, in such a way that only his heel remained vulnerable.

His two tutors were *Chiron*, the centaur, who taught him medicine, fighting, and hunting, and *Phoenix*, Amyntor's son, who taught him the art of discourse and the use of weapons. Moreover, he enjoyed the faithful friendship of *Patroclus*, *Menoetius'* son.

When Thetis knew that Ulysses and Nestor were coming in search of Achilles, she sent him to the court of King *Lycomedes*, where he dressed as a girl to pass unnoticed among the King's daughters. They called him 'Pyrrha', the blonde, and the Greek heroes couldn't find him until Ulysses thought of a trick to discover him. One version tells how, disguised as a peddler, he mixed mirrors, necklaces, and weapons and asked the girls to choose what they wanted as a present, and evidently, Achilles betrayed himself by choosing a sword. Another version tells how Ulysses simulated an attack on the palace; the daughters fled screaming, while Achilles alone stood up to them.

So Ulysses explained why he was there, and thanks to his smooth rhetoric, he managed to convince the young man, eager for adventures. After consulting an oracle, Thetis said that if he left he would have a short, glorious life, and if he stayed, he would enjoy a long, peaceful one. Achilles chose to follow his destiny, which is why he is the symbol of the warrior's valour, and left Thetis with tears in her eyes, since she knew he was to die beneath the walls of

Troy. However, she gave him the armour Hephaestus had made, and he received the protection of Hera and Athena.

VI. The Trojan War

The expedition of suitors named *Agamemnon*, Menelaus' brother, as supreme commander. They built the fleet for two years and recruited armies and other heroes. When everything was ready, they consulted the oracle, who declared they would not have favourable winds unless Agamemnon sacrificed his daughter, *Iphigenia*. Despite his grief and repugnance at such a sacrifice, but compelled by ambition, he deceived his daughter, saying she was going to marry Achilles. As he was about to sacrifice her, Artemis swapped her for a stag and took her to Tauris.

Having pacified the gods' anger, favourable winds grew, and the fleet left for Troas. But when they arrived at the Trojan coasts, no one wanted to get off the boat, because the oracle had predicted that the first warrior to disembark would meet instant death.

Protesilaus and Laodamia

Upon seeing that none of his companions would disembark, *Protesilaus,* one of the bravest leaders of the expedition, decided to sacrifice himself, and he energetically disembarked, dying beneath *Hector's* blows.

The news of his death reached his beloved wife, *Laodamia*, who was waiting patiently for him in Thessaly. Her heart was broken with grief, and between wails, she implored the gods not to be so cruel and to let her see him one last time. The love of both moved Zeus, and he ordered Hermes to carry the valiant warrior to be with his wife for three hours. The time flew by, and Protesilaus hardly had time to finish telling his wife what had happened. Then, Laodamia's heart stopped breaking, and Hermes took them both to the Elysian Fields.

* * *

The war between the Greeks and the Trojans then began
and lasted for nine long years, during which time both sides
demonstrated valour and courage. What happened there has
been the subject of many poems. Nevertheless, nearly all of
these focus on the last two years.

Chryseis and Briseis

In one of the many Greek skirmishes, they captured two
beautiful youths; *Chryseis,* daughter of *Chryses,* priest of
Apollo, and *Briseis.* The first was assigned to Agamemnon,
as reward for his bravery, and the second to Achilles. But
Chryses asked Apollo for vengeance, and he sent an epidemic that decimated the Greek troops. They consulted an
oracle, who told them the only way to pacify Apollo's ire
was by returning Chryseis to her father. Agamemnon
declared that he would only agree if Achilles also released
Briseis. He agreed, under pressure from everyone, but
swore not to take up arms ever again, and he shut himself
in his boat.

* * *

On one occasion, Hector, eldest son of Priam, proposed
the war be resolved in a single man-to-man combat
between the two men most interested in the battle, Paris
and Menelaus. The proposal was accepted by all, and the
two men began to fight. Half way through the fight,
Aphrodite saw that her protected mortal was about to die at
the hands of his enemy, so she wrapped him in a cloud and
took him to Helen's rooms, who bitterly reproached him his
cowardice.

After Paris' escape, the war restarted. Since Achilles
refused to fight, *Patroclus*, took up his armour and weapons
and threw himself into the battle. In spite of the magical
armour, forged by Hephaestus himself, Patroclus died in a

singular battle with Hector. When the sad news reached Achilles, inconsolable, he swore vengeance.

VII. Hector

Hector was the fiercest, most noble Trojan warrior and a model husband and father. This hero was married to the daughter of the King of Thebes in Mycenae, *Andromache*, with whom he had a single son, *Astyanax,* whom he adored. An oracle had foretold that Troy would not fall as long as Hector was alive. Protected by Apollo, he defeated many Greek heroes in one-to-one combat and was very admired and venerated by his compatriots. However, misfortune struck on the day he killed Patroclus, fuelling Achilles' anger.

Ignoring his wife and parents' pleas, Hector accepted the duel proposed by Achilles. The Trojan hero decided that he would rather die valiantly than live a cowardly life, and he accepted his destiny (since only Achilles could kill him), hoping for the protection of the gods. However, fate was not on his side, and Hector fell with his throat cut by Achilles' spear. Before dying, he asked the Greek hero to permit him a worthy burial. Contrary to this request, Achilles drilled a hole through his ankles and tied him to his chariot. At the Greek's refusal, Hector predicted that his death was also near.

Achilles drove nine times around the Trojan palace with the body of the noble Hector dragging along the dusty ground, while Hecuba, Priam, and Andromache watched in anguish and despair for the grief and the shame.

Achilles' death

Zeus sent Thetis to pacify Achilles' anger and to return the misfortunate Hector's body to his family. Later, Priam arrived accompanied by his beautiful daughter *Polyxena*. The father's pleas and the beauty of the sister softened the hero's heart, and he allowed them to take their beloved

Hector.

Hector's body. It is said that to conquer beautiful Polyxena's heart, Achilles, head over heels in love with her, proposed to Priam to either lay down his weapons and return with her to Greece or to join the Trojan side. When he was about to marry, Paris, who guided by Apollo had hidden in some nearby bramble, shot an arrow, which, thanks to the god's accurate blowing, fatally wounded the hero just in his vulnerable heel.

His prized armour was fiercely disputed for between Ulysses and *Ajax*, the Great, King of Salamina. Finally, the former made the magical armour his own, and Ajax, in a fit of madness, committed suicide. Meanwhile, according to another version, Polyxena committed suicide, inconsolable at the death of her fiancé, and according to another, she was sacrificed by *Neoptolemus*, son of Achilles, to pacify the latter's anger.

Paris' death

Then, as the oracle had predicted, the Greek victory came about when they found the arrows poisoned by Heracles, which were in *Philoctetes'* possession. He had witnessed Heracles' death, and his bow and arrows had been left to him. However, Philoctetes committed perjury and revealed where the hero's ashes could be found, for which he was punished. This punishment was enacted on the day the expedition, in which he participated as one of Helen's suitors, arrived at the island of Tenedos. There, he injured himself in his heel with one of his arrows.

The wound, apart from not healing, gave off such a stink that the Greeks abandoned him there. Ten years went by until Ulysses arrived, as ambassador, to ask that he return together with them. At first, his pride wounded, he refused, but Heracles revealed to him in his dreams that he would be cured in Troy by *Podalirius* and *Machaon*, sons of Asclepius. So it was, it was then told, that he took part in many fights and one of his arrows struck Paris.

Fatally wounded, Paris remembered his promise to Oenone, and he ordered her to be summoned. But she, offended by his abandoning her and jealous of Helen, refused to help him. However, a little later, she regretted her decision and ran to help her former lover. Unfortunately, it was too late, and she found Paris' funeral pyre; so she threw herself into the flames and burnt to death beside her great love.

* * *

The Greeks learnt that Troy would not fall as long as *Palladium* – a sacred statue to the goddess Athena – remained within the walls of the city. Ulysses and *Diomedes, Tydeus'* son and one of the most valiant Greek heroes along with the former, Achilles, or Ajax, managed to penetrate the city and take possession of the precious image.

The Trojan horse

Nevertheless, after ten years of siege, the Greeks had not managed to defeat the Trojans, who resisted valiantly. So Ulysses proposed a scheming stratagem to get inside the city and take it by surprise. Other versions suggest seers such as *Pryllis* or *Calchas*. Agamemnon ordered *Epeus* and *Panopeus* to make a large wooden horse. Although Epeus had the reputation of a being a coward, he was also renowned for his genius. They say that it was the goddess Athena who inspired him and guided him in the construction of the hollow horse, with a door sculpted in its side, through which Menelaus, Ulysses, Demophon, and up to fifty warriors entered.

The Greeks made it seem as if they were bored of the fighting and missed their homeland. They left the horse on the beach, lifted the siege, and set sail for Greece. However, they stopped at the island of Tenedos where they hid. Meanwhile, the astonished Trojans couldn't decide whether to leave the city or what to do with the horse.

Sinon, a wise slave, tricked the Trojans by saying that they should bring the horse into the city and keep it as a monument to their victory over the fleeing Greeks.

Cassandra opposed the entrance of the horse without success, since, as always, no one believed her. *Laocoon* supported Cassandra and even threw a javelin to prove that the horse was hollow.

Laocoon, son of the Trojan prince *Anthenor,* was a priest of Apollo (or Poseidon, according to another version). This wise priest's efforts to dissuade his compatriots were in vain, so that, as a last recourse, he decided to offer sacrifices to his god to get help. However, two enormous snakes came out of the ground and threw themselves on Laocoon and his two sons, who were helping him at the altar. The two beasts lashed their faces and strangled them.

The Trojans took this fact as a punishment for his opposition to letting the wooden horse into the city. As a result, they opened the gates of the city in pairs and brought the horse inside – and with it their downfall. When night fell, the Greek warriors abandoned their hiding place and opened the gates to the city, letting their companions, having returned, into the city. Then they invaded, killing, pillaging, and burning everything within their grasp. Not even the royal family was spared in the massacre.

* * *

Following the sacking, Agamemnon took Cassandra as loot. As it happened, he truly fell in love with her and made her mother of two children. Although Cassandra begged him to go back to Argos, since death was waiting for him, he did not believe her, and the four of them died at the hands of Clytemnestra and Aegisthus.

When Paris died, Helen was forced to marry *Deiphobus*, his younger brother. So the first thing Menelaus did was murder Deiphobus. At first, his meeting with his wife was dramatic. However, Helen's beauty, still maintained after ten years, softened Menelaus' heart, while he remembered the first years of the married life; he forgave her, and together they were reconciled. The return to Sparta was long and arduous. After eight years of travelling, they finally arrived in their homeland, where they enjoyed several years of total

Laocoon.

happiness until they both died. Helen was carried to the Elysian Fields, where she took Achilles as her husband.

When Achilles died, all the Nereid Thetis' affection landed on her grandson, Neoptolemus, whose life she saved by asking him not to return immediately to his country after the fall of Troy. That was how Neoptolemus saved himself from the great storm that destroyed the Greek fleet.

King Priam of Troy's end was hyperbolic. He sought refuge in the depths of his palace with his wife Hecuba, and they hugged at Zeus' altar. But Neoptolemus cut his throat. Hecuba was chosen as Ulysses' booty. Before being captured, the Queen had confided in her only living son, Polydorus, King of Chersonessus. However, she discovered the body of her son on the riverbank. Determined to get revenge, she summoned Polymnestor, King of Cherronessos. She tore out his eyes and killed his two children accompanying him. Polymnestor's subjects chased her to stone her, but just when they were about to catch her, she turned into a dog and leapt into the sea. The spot has been known since then as 'Cynossema' (tomb of the dog).

VIII. Ulysses' return

This hero's long, dangerous return voyage to his homeland is related by Homer in "The Odyssey". It was during this eternal return to Ithaca that Ulysses had the most passionate, heroic adventures of his life, since, among all the Greek leaders that returned to Greece, he was subjected to the greatest of the gods' anger.

After departing from sacked Troy, he was dragged by a storm to the coasts of the country of the *Cicones*, in Thrace, famous for their cruelty; after, fate had it that the winds took them to Libya, to the island of the *Lotus-eaters,* a plant that caused oblivion. Ulysses had to tie down the crew who had tried the magic plant and force them to leave the island.

Adrift in the sea, since they had lost all sense of direction thanks to the whims of the winds, they arrived at Sicily where the Cyclops lived. One of these monsters, *Polyphemus*, ate half the crew, but Ulysses managed to escape alive along with the rest of his men thanks to his genius and fast-thinking. First, he told the giant that his name was *Nobody*, then he offered him some wine, and once drunk, he ripped out his eye. His screams alerted his other companion Cyclops, but when they asked who had attacked him, he replied "Nobody!" So the Cyclops all walked off, and Ulysses was able to escape.

However, Polyphemus' father, Poseidon, wanted revenge for his son, and he caused an almighty storm. They managed to moor on the Aeolian Islands where lived Aeolus, the god of the winds, who offered to help Ulysses, gifting him with an ox-hide bag with the winds in his control. However, Ulysses' men believed the bag was full of gold, and they opened it, freeing all the winds at the same time and causing a great storm. They were thrown to the island of the *Lestrygonians,* a cannibalistic people they were able to flee from, but not before *Antiphates,* their king, had eaten some of them.

Later, Ulysses arrived at the island of Aeaea, where *Circe,* the great sorceress, lived. She transformed all the crew into pigs. However, Ulysses forced her to change them back into their original form, and spellbound by her beauty and pleasant company, he stayed with her long enough for her to have son with him, *Telegonus.* Before leaving, Circe advised him to visit *Tyresias,* the old seer, so that he would tell him the best way back to Ithaca. So he disembarked in the land of the *Cimmerians,* in whose regions the ocean flowed, marking the edges of the Earth. He penetrated the kingdom of Hades to consult the seer, who predicted he would arrive in Ithaca alone, and he would have to kill all his wife Penelope's suitors. Before leaving the underworld, the hero had the chance to see, for the last time, his mother *Anticlea,* who had died while he was fighting in Troy.

On his journey, he met the *Sirens*, who he avoided by blocking his crew's ears and having them tie him to the mast. Then he had to avoid two monsters: Charybdis and Scylla, who lived on two islands so close to each other that it was very difficult to avoid one without falling captive to the other. Finally, they arrived at the coasts of the island of

Thrinacia, where they committed the imprudence of eating some oxen from the god Aeolus' herd. As punishment, Zeus struck the impious with his lightning bolts and destroyed the boat in a storm.

Only Ulysses could save himself, and gripping a piece of wood, he arrived at the island of Ogygia, where he was looked after by the nymph *Calypso*. This beautiful nymph fell in love with the hero and kept him there for eight years. Finally, Athena begged Zeus to lift his punishment, and he sent his son Hermes to help Ulysses build a raft. After many days at sea, Poseidon, who still hadn't forgiven Ulysses, caused a storm and flung him onto the shore of the island of the *Phaeacians*. There, he was rescued by *Nausicaa,* daughter of *Alcinous*, King of the island, and *Alete*. Once recovered from his new shipwreck, he was hidden in the cabin of a Phaeacian boat and taken to Ithaca without Poseidon noticing.

Disguised as a beggar, he looked for his son *Telemachus,* who told him everything that had happened in his long absence. During those twenty years, the beautiful Penelope had rejected all the offers of marriage she had been offered. However, when the news arrived that Ulysses had perished, Penelope matched her husband's quick-thinking and declared that she would choose her new husband on the day she finished the tapestry she was weaving (or according to other mythologists, the funeral shroud for her father-in-law Laertes). During the night, she undid the tapestry she had woven during the day, until a servant revealed her strategy. She was on the point of finishing the tapestry when Ulysses appeared at the palace, and together with Telemachus, they killed all the suitors. Penelope was able to recognise her husband thanks to the scar on his knee, and they enjoyed a long night of love lengthened by Athena. She also impeded the family members of the suitors from seeking revenge.

Some versions tell how Ulysses died years later at the hands of Telegonus, who, unaware that the hero was his father, killed him with a javelin he had made from the bones of a ray fish. So it was that the prophecy was fulfilled that the hero would die at the hands of his son and the sea.

Penelope.

Analysis of the myth

Although it has always been thought that Homer's epics were purely legend, the archaeological investigations of the German archaeologist, Schliemann, proved, in 1870, that Troy really had existed in the place Homer related, between the banks of two rivers in Asia Minor, current-day Turkey, around the year 1184 BC.

Later, upon Schliemann's death, another archaeologist, Dorpfield, and his team, excavated on Hissarlik Hill in an attempt to prove the historical truth of the existence of Troy. They discovered that not only did one 'Troy' exist, but nine on top of each other. They deduced from the discovered remains the wars that had taken place and that the 7A layer, where they were able to find traces of fire, corresponded to Priam's reign. That is precisely the reason why, nowadays, it is not questioned whether or not, at the end of the thirteenth century BC, there was a great battle between Greek invaders and the native people of the land of Troas.

Located between the Black Sea and the Aegean and dominated by the Hellespont passage (today the Dardanelles Strait), Troy was situated in a strategic position, and throughout the second millennium BC, it had been very important at an economic (since, we presume, the Trojan kings made boats pay a toll for passing there), military, and cultural level. The theory that the Greeks formed an alliance to command this prized, coveted connecting place between Asia and Europe, is perhaps very close to the truth. Finally, it would appear that the city was destroyed by an earthquake.

The characteristics of the war, its long duration, likewise the consequences that followed, were a rich source of inspiration for the imagination of the Greek civilisation, bursting into an endless succession of myths and legends. It reaches us through masterpieces such as Homer's "The Iliad" or "The Odyssey" or Virgil's "The Aeneid". On the sidelines of these classic writers, there are also others, such as Shakespeare, Racine, or Joyce, in the field of literature, since this legend has also served as a source of inspiration for many other musical and artistic realms. Even the names of the heroes in this war have given names to the fifteen asteroids that form an equilateral triangle with Jupiter and the Sun.

As we have seen, the destiny of all these heroes was irremediably marked by foreseen, divine paths. Aside from this characteristic, the heroes were differentiated from other mortals for a series of reasons: first their births, since they are born miraculously, and often in humble circumstances, and they generally are sired by gods or divinities, who, in the course of their life, protect and help them; during their childhood, they already distinguish themselves for their valour and courage, and in their adolescence, they tend to live a tragic life, caused by the conflict of Good and Evil; finally, they are distinguished by some features of extraordinary physical and moral strength, accumulating deed upon deed with great daring, which raises them above their fellow beings and brings them closer to the gods.

Each Greek territory or region had its own hero. However, although they were adored almost as gods, the Greek heroes lived marked by a terrible destiny that made them victims either of the betrayals of people or by some divine decision that, for some reason, sought to punish them.

In the Trojan War, there is *Agamemnon*, who stood out for his majesty and dignity; although he wasn't thought of as a hero, in the ancient meaning of the word, he was a worthy representative of the Achaean race that built Greece. *Ulysses*, above all, was thought of as the symbol of quick-thinking and genius; thanks to his courage and eloquence, he was able to overcome all sorts of dangers and threats he found himself subjected to throughout his life. Ulysses was the prototype of the hero with whom the Greeks liked to identify themselves most of all. And his return to his homeland was symbolic of the eternal return, an example of the pilgrimage of human life. Achilles was a symbol of bravery; the ideal of friendship, ferocity, and sense of chivalry, he always enjoyed the Greek nation's sympathy.

On the Trojan side, *Priam* stands out for his paternalistic feeling, as well as his majesty; but, above all, *Hector*, considered in ancient times to be the model of filial, conjugal piety, likewise was a model of valour and generosity for having preferred death to the slavery of defeat. Apart from Priam and Hector, we should emphasise the dignity of the Trojan women, such as *Hecuba* and *Andromache,* models of conjugal fidelity and the bonding of the nation. Among the Greek heroines, there was the controversial *Helen,* victim or guilty party, which raises the issue of responsibility for the start of the Trojan War. Homer presented her as an instrument of destiny, due to her irresistible beauty. Hesiod and Aeschylus presented her as a destructive force. Finally, the Romans presented her to us as the model of the light, passive woman.

On the other hand, patient *Penelope* has become the symbol of conjugal fidelity, even more emphasised by the scarcity of such a quality among the other wives of heroes who left to go to the Trojan War.

V APPENDICES

CLASSIFICATION OF MYTHS
(According to content)

1. COSMOGONIC:

Attempt to explain the origin of the world.

2. THEOGONIC:

An account of the origin of the gods.

3. ANTHROPOGENIC:

Aim to explain the origin and development of humans.

4. ETHYOLOGICAL:

An attempt to explain the reason for specific political, social, or religious institutions.

5. ESCHATOLOGICAL:

Referring to life after death or the end of the world.

6. MORALISTIC:

Tending to refer to the struggle between contrary principles: good and evil; the angel and the devil.

At times, in a single myth, there might be a mix of two or more of these elements, or none of them, as there are some that can't be adapted to this classification.

LITERARY SOURCES OF MYTHOLOGY

AUTHOR	YEAR	WORKS
Homer	Around 800 BC	Iliad / Odyssey
Hesiod	Around 725 BC	Theogony Works and Days
Aeschylus	Around 525-456 BC	Prometheus Bound Oresteia: Agamemnon, The Libation Bearers, The Eumenides / Seven Against Thebes
Sophocles	496-405 BC	Antigone / Electra / Oedipus Rex
Herodotus	Around 484-420 BC	The History of Herodotus
Euripides	480-406 BC	Medea / Hippolytus / Madness of Heracles / Women of Troy / Electra / Orestes / Bacchanals / The Cyclops / Helen
Callimachus	?	Hymns to: Zeus, Apollo, Artemis / The Argonauts
Apollodorus	Around 150 BC	On the gods
Catullus	Around 87-54 BC	Elegies: The Wedding of Peleus and Thetis / Berenice's Hair
Virgil	71-19 BC	The Bucolics / The Aeneid
Ovid	43 BC - 17 AD	Metamorphoses / Fasti
Seneca	4-65 AD	Hercules Enraged / Trojan Women / Medea / Phaedra / Oedipus / Agamemnon / The Phoenicians
Plutarch	Around 50-125 AD	Parallel Lives
Apuleius	125- about 180 AD	Metamorphoses

HEROIC GENEALOGIES

I. PERSEUS AND HERACLES

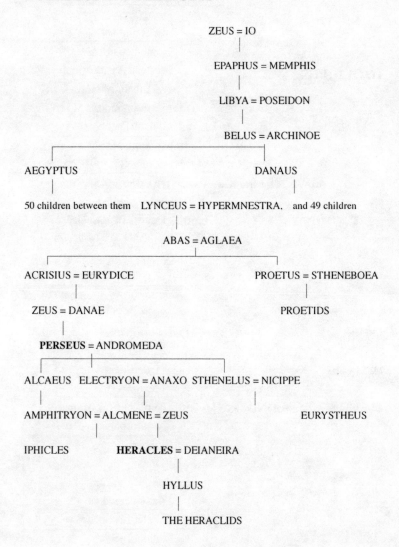

ZEUS = IO

EPAPHUS = MEMPHIS

LIBYA = POSEIDON

BELUS = ARCHINOE

AEGYPTUS   DANAUS

50 children between them   LYNCEUS = HYPERMNESTRA,   and 49 children

ABAS = AGLAEA

ACRISIUS = EURYDICE   PROETUS = STHENEBOEA

ZEUS = DANAE   PROETIDS

PERSEUS = ANDROMEDA

ALCAEUS   ELECTRYON = ANAXO   STHENELUS = NICIPPE

AMPHITRYON = ALCMENE = ZEUS   EURYSTHEUS

IPHICLES   **HERACLES** = DEIANEIRA

HYLLUS

THE HERACLIDS

II. OEDIPUS

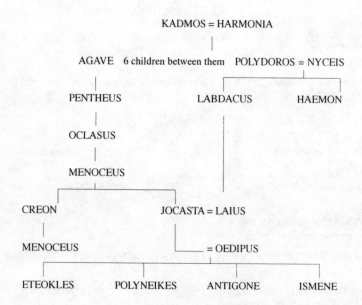

III. ORESTES AND ELECTRA

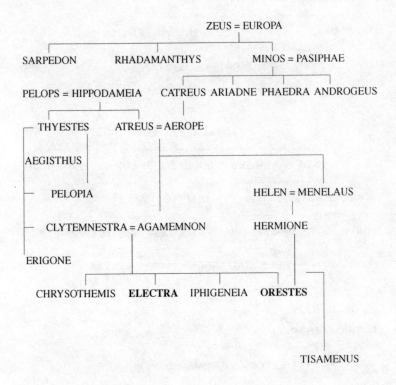

IV. TROJAN

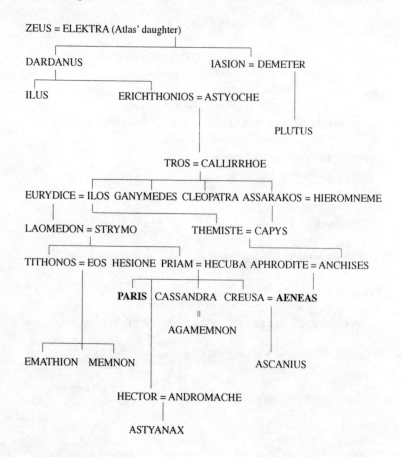

ZEUS = ELEKTRA (Atlas' daughter)

DARDANUS

IASION = DEMETER

ILUS

ERICHTHONIOS = ASTYOCHE

PLUTUS

TROS = CALLIRRHOE

EURYDICE = ILOS   GANYMEDES   CLEOPATRA   ASSARAKOS = HIEROMNEME

LAOMEDON = STRYMO

THEMISTE = CAPYS

TITHONOS = EOS   HESIONE   PRIAM = HECUBA   APHRODITE = ANCHISES

PARIS | CASSANDRA   CREUSA = **AENEAS**
||
AGAMEMNON

EMATHION   MEMNON

ASCANIUS

HECTOR = ANDROMACHE

ASTYANAX

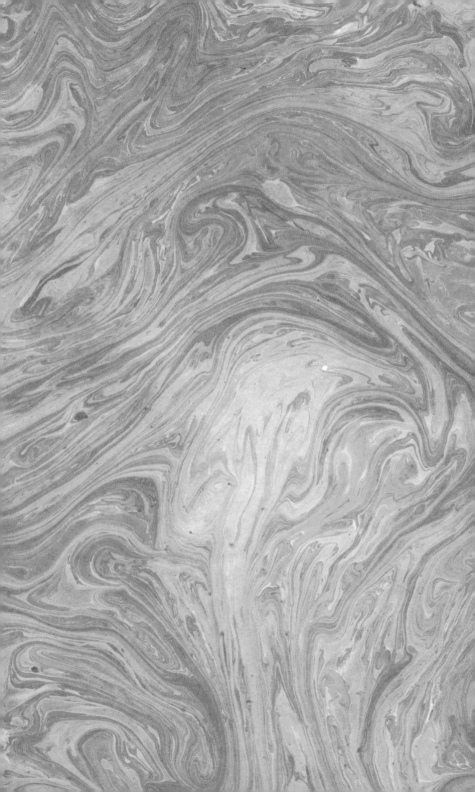